I0777902

# PRINCE OF THE ARENA

## BEASTS OF THE BRIAR

### ELIZABETH HELEN

LUNA FOX
PRESS

Prince of the Arena

Copyright © 2025 by Elizabeth Helen

All rights reserved.



Published by Luna Fox Press LTD

First Edition published June 2025

Interior Design © 2025 by Elizabeth Helen

Cover Design and Illustration © 2025 by saintjupit3rgr4phic

Ch. 10 and 20 illustrations © elisegcreativity

Identifiers

ISBN: 978-1-998945-10-8 (eBook)

ISBN: 978-1-998945-09-2 (paperback)

ISBN: 978-1-998945-11-5 (audio)

*To Buttercup, Westley, Luna, Suki, and Sokka,*
*Meow meow. Meow meow meow purrrrrr, meow meow. Meow meow meow.*
*Meow.*
*(Translation: To our most wonderful cats, who we love endlessly. Thank you for the cuddles, the laughs, and your infinite feline wisdom.)*

# AUTHORS' NOTE

*Prince of the Arena* is an adult fantasy book. It contains mature themes, including M/M content, and is intended for audiences 18+.

It is a prequel novella that takes place many years before the events of the *Beasts of the Briar* series. It is best enjoyed after reading *Bonded by Thorns*.

# PART ONE
# THE MEETING

# I

# DAYTON

"I'd rather slice off my own cock than have anything to do with that boring, pasty-faced, quill-brained Autumn Prince."

Muscles clench in Damocles's jaw as he no doubt nearly bites his tongue off to stop himself from an equally crude retort. My eldest brother detests vulgar language, especially in Soltide Keep.

I find it hard to get my point across without it.

The High Prince of Summer sits straight-backed on the Coral Throne, his golden crown catching the last slanting rays of the setting sun. A misty evening breeze drifts in from the large open windows that lead to the sea, carrying the briny scent of salt and distant storms. I wish I could be out there now, swimming or sailing on my skiff. Anywhere but in this prison of a room.

The Coral Throne is a monstrous thing—twisting, spiraling columns of deep pink and bloodred coral fused together, half-grown, half-constructed. It looks torn from the ocean's depths rather than built for a ruler. Jagged edges glisten with seawater, and tiny pearls gleam in the rough coral, embedded like captured stars. The back curves high overhead, a tangled lattice of ivory and shell, casting strange, netlike shadows across the marble.

I shift where I stand, uncomfortable just looking at it. Damocles graces it as if it were made for him. I suppose it was in a way. If I sat there, the coral would probably bite into my skin. But not him. The throne and the prince suit each other—beautiful, sharp, and impossible to grasp without bleeding. Especially when my brother summons me for one of his terrible ideas.

"Daytonales," Damocles says, always sure to use my full name, "it is far past time you take your position in this family seriously. Farron is heir to Autumn's Blessing, and you, as a third-born son, would be smartly matched to him."

I don't bother hiding my groan—there's no one around to hear it. Damocles always clears out the court before these talks, as if he expects me to say something stupid and shatter his prestigious reputation.

"High Princess Niamh has nothing but praise for her son," Damocles continues. "She says he is a studious—"

"Boring."

"Compassionate—"

"Bleeding heart."

"Prudent—"

"Spineless."

"—young man." Damocles's jaw clenches harder. "Though she wishes he would find a companion."

"So, is that what you and the High Princess were scheming about when you visited Coppershire last month?"

"Being consort to a High Ruler is a privilege. Once Farron inherits Autumn's Blessing, you would reside in Castletree itself."

"Still right beside you, brother." I flash him a smile. *How you would love to keep me under your ever-watchful eye, Dammy.* "If it's such an honor, then why not give it to your heir, Decimus?"

"Decimus is Imperator of the Summer's Legionnaires. This duty keeps him busy enough."

*And out of trouble,* I finish the unspoken words in my head. Not that the middle brother of Summer has ever caused a stir for Damocles.

"Besides," Damocles continues, "Decimus does not fancy men."

"And this Autumn Prince does?"

"That remains unclear. Though Niamh and I theorized that if anyone could determine such a thing, it would be you. It appears the prince's past romances have been limited."

"So, he's boring and a loser?"

"Daytonales, that is inappropriate talk for a Blessing's heir. You have not seen the High Prince since you were both younglings."

"Right, I might have *accidentally* splashed him with a wave and got a little water on his book, which he hadn't put down the entire festival. He called me a hideous toad and ran away crying. Doesn't look like a match fated in the stars."

Damocles lets out a long sigh, and I study him. It's like staring into a cursed sort of mirror, because while we share so many features, I could never imagine myself looking similar to him. He stands stiff as a statue, with cropped golden hair, a permanent straight line for a mouth, tan but never burned skin, and robes that don't even have a whisper of a wrinkle. On a chain around his neck hangs a gleaming shell: the token of Summer that signifies his status as High Ruler. With that little charm, he can return to Castletree from anywhere in the Vale.

Now, *that* is interesting.

"Daytonales, this is not an arrangement nor a duty, but it is a prospect you should seriously consider for your future."

"Seriously consider? Seriously, Dammy?" I spread my arms wide and step back. "You know I don't understand what the word *future* means."

He breaks my gaze and massages the bridge of his nose. "Be presentable for the Autumn Royal Family's arrival this afternoon. I expect you to be on your best behavior for the welcome gala tonight."

"Of course, High Prince." I turn without waiting for a formal dismissal.

Outside the throne room, I slip out of a window and down a rocky ledge to stare at the foaming water breaking upon the shore.

*A prospect you should seriously consider for your future.*

Damocles thinks the future means court and politics, rules, and meetings. Trapped in a tree where you don't fall asleep to the sound of waves.

No, my future isn't there.

My future is the oceans, the grand horizon, and, of course, the sands of the arena.

# 2

## FARRON

The marble floor is so perfectly polished, I can see my reflection in it like a pond. If only it were made of water, I could sink straight to the bottom and never emerge.

I'm no stranger to parties. I often travel with my family throughout Autumn, celebrating harvest and new moon festivals. Not to mention, my book club at the Scriptorium can get positively raucous at our year-end celebration. Why, last time, Professor Thiran even cracked open his aged single malt whiskey, and we all took a nip. By night's end, we were poring over poetry about falling stars and tide-kissed sailors. Certainly not the work of scholars. Ah, wild times.

But parties in the Summer Realm are a completely different beast. Here at Soltide Keep, the heart of Hadria, men and women saunter through the ballroom, sashaying by coral-encrusted pillars wearing less clothing than I do when I'm merely in my undergarments. Mother insisted we dress per their customs. My father, Padraig, embraced it; I catch sight of him now, juggling three pomegranates for a wide-eyed crowd of Summer children. His barrel chest, smothered in bright red hair, is on display, barely contained by the rivers of white cloth draped over one shoulder.

I subconsciously pull at my own clothing, a sheet of swathed orange fabric, wishing it covered more of my pale chest. Despite it not being the custom, I did, in fact, keep my undergarments *on*.

Soltide Keep, I must admit, is truly an architectural marvel. It's no wonder it's also known as the Summer Palace; it appears designed for beauty rather than fortitude. The palace is crafted of organic sea matter with bones of stucco, plaster, and colored tiles that form gorgeous mosaics. Though the floor is marble, the pillars and ceilings are the lightest pink, appearing as if cut from coral. Glistening tide pools are carved into alcoves, smelling of briny ocean and filled with all manner of sea stars, barnacles, and seagrasses.

It's gloriously cool within the palace, despite the heat outside. The season never changes in the four realms: the Summer Realm is always blistering hot, Winter cold and unyielding, Spring fragrant and green, and my own Autumn Realm is always crisp and colored in a cornucopia of reds, yellows, oranges, and browns. But all the realms observe the annual calendar, which is based on the seasons around Castletree —the only place in the Enchanted Vale blessed to experience all four seasons.

I imagine Castletree is beautiful right now, basking in warm sun and balmy breezes through the glorious meadows and forests that surround it.

Servants stroll through the ballroom holding platters of food, including bread baked with olives, palm leaves stuffed with figs and dates, and even sea urchins, still with their spines. I don't dare attempt one of those, but I do help myself to two honeyed custards and a glass of saffron wine.

I know Mother wants me to mingle with everyone—*especially* the Summer Royal Family—but my feet are planted to the floor. Thankfully, no one has wandered over and attempted to make conversation with me. I purposely chose my location to blend in: surrounding me are pedestals adorned with marble busts, depicting the previous High Rulers of Summer as well as famed gladiators, sailors, and artists.

"Great party, isn't it?" I turn to the bust right beside me. The man's marble eyes stare back, emotionless yet piercing. "Come here often"— I peer down at the plaque below the bust—"Aeneas?" Aeneas, the first High Prince of Summer, does not respond. The perfect company for a party. "So, how about the honeyed custards?" I nudge the pedestal with my elbow as if we're old friends. The movement makes the bust wobble, and with a yelp, I snatch Aeneas's skull and steady him. A servant gives me a stern glare as she passes by with more goblets of wine.

Sighing, I mumble, "I'm hopeless."

Even my baby sister isn't as pathetic as I am. Princess Eleanor, our sweet Nori, despite barely being of age to attend school, is peering over a tide pool and pointing at the various treasures within. Though I can't hear what she's saying, I know she's likely reciting memorized facts to her captive audience and apparent chaperone for the evening, Prince Decimus of Summer.

I search my memory for everything I know of the Royal Family. Decimus is the middle child, an accomplished gladiator and the Imperator of Summer's army. His mother, Princess Sabine, married twice, first to Cenarius, a bard-warrior, then to Ovidius, a famous navigator and naval commander. Having multiple spouses is not unusual in the Enchanted Vale, though certainly it is more common in Summer than in Autumn.

Decimus is sired by Ovidius, I recall. They share the same dark brown skin and prowess with a short sword, but where Ovidius wears his hair in long braids and boasts an impressive beard, Decimus's hair is shorn, his face clean-shaven. Despite Decimus's fearsome reputation in the arena, he appears to be endlessly patient with Nori, nodding as she rambles on about her tide pool findings.

Even my brothers are honoring Mother's wishes to mingle. Dominic and Billagin—imps disguised as boys—have cozied up next to the warriors Ovidius and Cenarius and are attempting their own gladiator match against one another, using skewers from the fruit plates. Like Decimus, the prince consorts show incredible patience. I watch as Ovidius puts his hands on their shoulders to correct their form, while Cenarius, a bronze-skinned man with a wild tangle of blond hair, laughs and cheers beside them.

Princess Sabine, the matriarch of the family, wanders over to watch this mock gladiator match, and my pulse rages in my ears. Our family has visited Hadria before and hosted their Royal Family in Coppershire, but the sight of Sabine never fails to make my heart quicken. With her blond hair braided into an elaborate crown upon her head, skin tanned from days in the sun, and eyes like aquamarines, she's beautiful as the dawn. Legends of sirens flutter through my mind, though I don't imagine any creature could be as lovely as she.

Sabine jumps between Dominic and Billagin, wielding her own skewer, and both her husbands laugh. After a valiant attempt to waylay my young brothers, Sabine allows them to strike the final blows and collapses to the ground in a dramatic display. Sabine was once a High Princess like my mother before she passed the rule to her eldest son. I try to conceive of my mother engaging in play of such a sort, but find my imagination lacking.

Last, I search the room for the rest of the members in attendance from both the Autumn and Summer houses. I'm not surprised to find them together, huddled in a corner, gossiping like old maids.

High Prince Damocles of Summer and High Princess Niamh of Autumn. My mother.

Though Damocles takes after his biological father, Cenarius, they do not appear to have much in common. Where Cenarius has a constant smile on his face, eyes crinkled with laughter, Damocles looks carved of stone. He wears a draping of dark blue cloth around his hips, leaving his chest bare. His shoulders are wide and thickly muscled, skin various shades of tan, most likely from training with equipment. He runs a hand over his shorn blond hair, and my mother leans closer to whisper to him.

Then they both direct their gazes at me.

My heart sinks. I can feel their piercing stares and even more piercing intentions from across the room. I know what they're whispering about. Mother couldn't keep silent about it for even five minutes while on our journey here.

They're trying to set me up with the third son of Summer.

*Daytonales.*

The name sends my blood boiling. I met him once, when we were both children, but that was enough to solidify my understanding of the youngest child of Sabine and Cenarius.

Daytonales is a hideous toad.

Back then, he was wild, crazy, careless. A tornado with tangled blond hair that smelled of the sea. He had no patience, no decorum, and no care for fine literature. I can only imagine what kind of brute the years have turned him into. All I know is he's made a name for himself as a gladiator, but he obviously hasn't learned manners, as he didn't even show up to greet us today with the rest of his family. If Mother thinks I'd have any interest in him, she doesn't understand me at all.

If my heart was in a pit, it sinks down to the Below as I watch Mother detach from Damocles's side and saunter over to me. I sigh and shift from foot to foot, desperately wishing I had another honeyed custard so I would have something to do with my hands.

"My clove, are you enjoying the party?" Mother grabs my arm and nuzzles against me. Her dark hair, woven into a long braid, shimmers with a few streaks of gray. Now that we're arm in arm, both dressed in the one-shouldered draped cloth of Summer, I notice how ghastly pale we are compared to the sun-loving Summer folk.

"Not as much as you seem to be," I mutter.

She flicks her gaze back to where Damocles stands. "The High Prince is quite a fine young man, isn't he? Apparently, he's already cleared the pirate blockade that plagued the Balthazar Isles for years. Isn't that impressive? Sabine was wise indeed, both to raise such a son and in her choice to pass the Blessing to him."

Oh no. Please don't let this be going where I think it's going. "Always seemed a bit soon for Sabine to pass her Blessing, don't you think? She's not even old." I chance a glance back at the Summer Princess, who is licking the juice of a pomegranate off her finger.

"Oh, she received the Blessing when she was very young. Had her fill of it. Besides, it's the right choice. We fae live too long to rule for our whole lives. No one should have this amount of power for such a lengthy time." She digs her fingers into my arm. "Fresh ideas! Young minds! The tenacity of youth. That's what society needs to flourish."

She looks up at me with a gaze too intense, but her voice becomes pensive. "For the sake of the Vale, we must pass power to the next generation."

This *is* going where I feared. Quickly, I say with a grin, "Good thing you don't look a day over three hundred."

Mother doesn't fall for the compliment. Instead, she shifts in front of me, taking my face in both her hands. "Sabine saw something in Damocles. We spoke of it at the last Council of the Realms. Isidora, Sabine, Erivor, and I. We four High Rulers have overseen times of turmoil and times of peace. It will only be a matter of time before Isidora passes her rule to her heir. Stagnation is the burden of civilization. For peace and prosperity, we must be growing, learning. It is only right that our reigns pass to those with the will and courage to act. Farron, you are smart and kind and—"

*And out of here,* I think, pulling away from my mother. "Must we do this now? Isn't it enough you're scheming with Damocles to set me up with his half-feral brother?"

Mother puts her hands on her hips. "Perhaps that's what you need. Someone to push you to do the hard things. Stars know I've never been capable of changing your stubborn mind. Daytonales may take taming, to be sure, but imagine it, Farron. You, on the throne of Coppershire, a High Ruler with a prince consort of royal Summer blood—"

Throne. High Ruler. A prince consort. Blood.

It's too much, it's all too much. My heart leaps into a gallop, and black creeps along the edges of my vision. Unable to take a full breath, I stagger backward, smacking into the bust of Aeneas, the first High Prince of Summer. With horror, I turn to see the bust wobbling back and forth. Both my mother and I let out cries and lunge for it, but it's too late. The bust clatters to the ground, shattering into a thousand pieces of marble.

The music stops. All voices cut off mid-word. The only sound is my raging heartbeat. Slowly, I turn back to the crowd to see every single pair of eyes staring at me.

Oh no. Oh nonononono.

I can't do this. I can't be here. I can't even make it through a party and Mother wants me to be *High Prince*?

What would she do in this scenario? Give a speech of apology? What about my father? Make some joke that would defuse the situation?

I have neither the charisma nor the charm. There's only one option.

Run.

Sprinting out of the ballroom, I careen down the nearest hallway. I take corner after corner with no mind to where I'm going. I need to get away from their gazes, my mother's horrified gasp. How does she not see what a mess I am? She's been hinting for the last year that she wants to pass the Blessing, but now she's full-on telling me that's the plan. I'm not ready.

I don't think I ever will be.

How do I get out of this blasted keep? I can't go through the main doors without crossing the ballroom, and I'll never show my face there again. I'm sure Mother's hunting me down right now, and my guest chamber will be the first place she'll look.

A briny breeze drifts down the hallway, and I catch sight of a curtain blowing in the wind. An open window. I rush to it. There's no plan, only the certainty that I can't be *here* anymore. Maybe I can flee to the marketplace and lose myself in the crowds. Or perhaps make my way back to Autumn. Stars, I'll swim if I have to.

I brace myself on the windowsill and take a deep breath of sea air.

I don't want to be a High Prince. And I *certainly* don't want to see the gladiator Prince of Summer.

Desperate to escape, I fling myself out of the window...and straight into the muscled chest of someone climbing in.

# 3

## DAYTON

A force hits me, and I fall to the ground with a hard *smack*. There's another fae on top of me.

"What in the bloody seven realms?" I croak, the breath knocked out of me.

The last thing I expected when trying to sneak into the gala—through the window, of course, because then Damocles couldn't prove I arrived late—was to be pushed from the window by a clumsy fool.

I grip the other fae by the shoulders and easily flip him onto his back. A thatch of wavy auburn hair falls across his brow, and he blinks up at me with huge golden eyes.

"Who are you?" I say, meaning my words to come out as a growl, but they get caught in my throat.

"P-please let me go," he cries. "I have nothing of value on me!"

I sit back on my heels and tilt my head. "What do you take me for? A thief?"

The young man takes a few shaking breaths, then sits up. "Who else would be climbing through the window of a keep?"

"And who would be climbing *out* of a window?" I take in his orange toga. Beneath, his skin is near translucent. This is no fae of the Summer Realm. "I know exactly who you are."

He staggers to his feet. "Y-you do?"

Standing, I flash him a grin. "A servant of Autumn escaping his duties. Do our festivities pale compared to your realm?"

His face blanches. "I don't need to explain myself to you, a dirty thief. In fact, I should report you."

I give myself a quick sniff. So, I'm not at my most presentable. Sand is still stuck to my skin, and my hair is salt crusted. I take a step toward him. "You're not going to do that, Little Leaf." I flick the golden leaf-shaped cuff over his pointed ear. "Because then you'll have to admit you were running away—"

"I wasn't running away!" A flush stains his freckled cheeks. "I needed some air. If you're not a thief, then who are you?"

"You could say I serve the realm in my own way."

The boy looks me up and down. He must decide I'm not an immediate threat to the realm, as he turns and begins to walk through the gardens surrounding the palace.

I look back at the window, where vines crawl up toward the glowing yellow light. I follow a few steps after the servant. "So, where are you going?"

"I'm going to take a quick loop around the keep before returning to my duties."

I huff out a breath. "That's so incredibly boring. If you're going to shirk your duties, you should at least have a bit of fun."

"This is enough for me," he says. "I'm not usually so impulsive."

I whistle through my teeth. "Wow, a garden walk. Positively shocking, Little Leaf."

He stops and shoots me a glare. Suddenly, I realize this Autumn servant has no idea who I am. Even though, as Damocles puts it, I dress like "a common goat herder" most of the time, I'd be hard-pressed to find a citizen of Summer who wouldn't recognize me on sight, much less have the nerve to shoot me a look like that.

"You know," I say, snatching his jaw with my hand, "that glare would be a lot more intimidating if it wasn't so cute."

His face flushes deeper, and he grips my wrist. "Let me go."

I don't. "What's your name?"

"Far—" He swallows. "Fare."

"That's cute too."

He pushes on my wrist again, and this time, I let him go. He walks a few paces away before glancing over his shoulder. "What's your name?"

"You can call me Day."

"Day," he repeats, keeping those captivating eyes on me.

Turning, I step on the path toward the city. "Hey, Fare," I call. "You can continue your little garden walk, or you could come with me, and I'll show you what a good time Hadria truly is."

He pauses, chest moving with his heavy breath. "I don't know you. Besides, weren't you trying to get into the gala?"

I look back at the glowing window. I know everything that awaits me in there: Damocles's judgmental gaze, being told by Decimus how pitiful my performance was in a recent spar, and awkward small talk with all those stuffy Autumn folk.

My gaze narrows on the boy in front of me. Maybe they aren't all so bad.

"I already got what I came for."

He shakes his head. "I don't know."

"Come on, Little Leaf." I hold out my hand. "Be impulsive for once in your life."

"Fare, hurry!" I inch through the narrow tunnel, my shoulders brushing the rough stone. The air is cool, a stark contrast to the humidity of the city. "This is the second to last thing I have to show you."

Fare grunts, following behind me. "I don't know how it could top the man who pretended his monkey could talk."

I shoot him a glare over my shoulder. "Celer *did* speak."

A laugh bubbles out of Fare, a sound I've quickly come to enjoy. "I already told you; the vendor was throwing his voice. He certainly didn't deserve your coin."

"Oh, but sweet Celer did, even if he tried to bite my poor fingy."

Fare laughs harder, and I can't help but join in.

So far tonight, I've managed to provide this little Autumn Leaf with quite the tour of Hadria.

Our first stop was to grab a couple of cloaks. I claimed they were for his protection—runaway servant that he is—though truthfully, I don't think anyone would care about that. What I don't want is for a citizen of Summer to recognize me and freak him out.

Because I've come to learn *everything* freaks him out.

The scorpions that scuttle across the road? He yelped and grabbed my arm.

The smell of garum repulsed him, even after I devoured two helpings of the saucy fish.

And his face went completely red when we walked past the public baths and he saw a bounty of naked fae inside. I'd be lying if I said his reactions didn't amuse me though. It was like seeing my city for the first time.

He enjoyed the market, somehow devouring four Libum cakes, his lips glistening with golden honey after. He found the arena intriguing as he watched through the window, but his particular interest lay in the architecture—the way the marble was shaped, and the legends carved into the walls.

I have to admit, no matter how many times I've walked through those halls, I've never seen it quite like I did with him.

But he lit up at the Dockside Book Forum. It's located in a rougher section of the city, where vendors have all converted their little boats and rafts into bookstores. I suppose being studious must be an Autumn trait, because not only did we have to buy a bag, but it took no time at all for Fare to fill it to the brim.

I swear he chose the heaviest damn tomes, because my shoulder is aching with the weight of this thing across my chest.

"We're almost there," I call back, adjusting the book bag and crawling forward. The tunnel bends sharply, and I twist my body to follow its path. My fingers dig into the rocky floor. Magic pulses ahead, a faint thrumming. The darkness is nearly all-encompassing, save for the occasional glint of mineral in the stone, reflecting the light from the small, glowing orb that bobs before us.

A handy spell of Fare's. If only it hadn't taken him forever to find the right scroll for the incantation in his pocket.

Eventually, the way widens, revealing a faint glow ahead. My heart quickens as I push myself faster, ignoring the sting of scrapes and bruises. The tunnel opens up and I jump out, blocking the entrance with my body as Fare approaches.

His face nearly bumps into my chest.

"Would you be freaked out if I told you to close your eyes?" I ask.

He lets out a soft breath. "Well, I can only assume the reason is my imminent demise, so—"

"Close your eyes, Fare."

He does. I swipe my hand through his glowing orb until it disperses into a misty haze.

"You're going to have to trust me, okay?"

Fare scoffs but allows me to help him out of the tunnel. The way his body melds to mine as I guide him over the uneven stone... *He does trust me. A man he just met.*

What an idiot. But a strange protectiveness surges through me, and I tug him a little closer.

"So, what's my death going to be?" Fare muses. "Thrown from a ledge? Sacrificed to an ancient deity of Summer? Drowned by selkies?"

Leaning down, my lips brush his ear, and it twitches. "Oh, Little Leaf, I've got something much more dastardly planned."

"I have no doubt."

I keep a hand in his as I say, "Open your eyes."

He does.

I watch closely as his expression changes. Flickering lights play over his skin. The walls are alive with bioluminescence, glowing in shades of blue and green that dance and shimmer like stars. The glow reflects off an underground lake, casting rippling patterns across the ceiling. Stalactites drip with crystalline water that catches the light.

"Wow." Fare's eyes are wide, his mouth open in awe. "This is incredible."

He steps toward one of the walls but doesn't let go of my hand. In fact, he squeezes it tighter. I smile, watching his curiosity take over. He studies the glowing patches intently, fingers hovering above the surface.

"I don't know what it is," I say, "but it sure is pretty."

"I've read about this type of cave before." Fare smiles, his eyes still fixed on the luminous patterns. "It's a combination of bioluminescent fungi and a special mineral on the rock walls. The fungi feed on the minerals, creating this radiant essence. It's a symbiotic relationship, one that's been here for centuries. Perhaps since the Queen created the Vale."

"Radiant essence," I repeat. "I call it blue goo."

Fare chuckles. "It's like nature's own magic."

"It's cold to the touch," I say, casting him a mischievous grin.

"You've *touched* it? Without even knowing if it was safe?"

I laugh, dipping my fingers into the blue goo—radiant essence—and pulling away a handful of the shimmering substance. "I was curious. But it hasn't harmed me yet."

Fare's eyes sparkle. He mimics my action, his fingers coming away coated in the glowing goo. He studies his luminous fingertips, then turns to me, a grin spreading across his face.

I swipe a finger along his shoulder, leaving a swirling blue line.

For a moment, I think he's going to be cross, but then he bites his lip and reaches up, tracing along my jaw. It's cold and a little tingly. I unclasp his cloak and tug down the shoulder of his orange toga, the fabric still wrapped around his waist.

"I wouldn't call myself an artist," I say, creating a sun on his chest, "but you make the most striking canvas."

His heartbeat races under my palm. He's thin, but as I glide my makeshift paint along his body, I can feel the lean muscles beneath.

Dipping his chin, he tracks my every movement before breaking into a shaky smile. "You are a terrible artist."

"Never insult a genius while he's working." I trace a circle around his belly button, then lower, over a small thatch of hair that dips beneath his toga.

His breath hitches, and he clasps my arm. "My turn."

"By all means." I drop my cloak to the ground. "I shall give you the most splendid canvas. In fact, I'm willing to be entirely nude."

Even in the dim light, I notice his cheeks reddening. "Uh, no. This will be more than enough space. Go sit by the water."

I do as I'm instructed and watch as Fare scoops a palmful of radiant essence. He dumps it into a pile beside me.

"Now, you have to close your eyes," he says.

I do and dissolve into the feeling of his hands over my chest. I think he might be using the water to dilute some of the paint as he glides and wisps it across my body. His warm breath caresses my skin as he leans closer.

"I should have brought my reading glasses," he mumbles. I crack a lid open, seeing his brow furrowed in concentration. He shoots me a glare. "I'm not finished."

His hand covers my eyes, but he effortlessly slides his fingers down my face, thumb brushing my lips. A strange anticipation prickles through me. A new feeling.

With my previous lovers, the intent was always there from the start. We'd fuck and it would be fabulous. I don't do...whatever this is.

Because this boy can't become a lover. It's one thing to ignore Damocles's request that I court the Autumn Prince. It would be like spitting in his face to fuck one of the Autumn Realm's staff. As much as I *love* annoying my eldest brother, there are some lines I can't cross.

No matter how good Fare's hands feel on my body. No matter how I can't help imagining him touching other parts of me, the sounds he would make as I enter him, the expression on his face as I trace those freckles on his nose with my tongue.

"Can I open my eyes yet?" I rasp.

"Almost done."

His fingers move in slow, deliberate strokes, and I hiss as he passes over one of my nipples.

"Sorry," he gasps.

"Don't be sorry. Just do it again."

I hear his sharp inhale. "Done."

"Shame." I keep my eyes closed, pitying the fact he's stopped touching me. "Sure you don't want to paint the rest of me while you're all gooey?"

"You don't even know if you like it."

Reluctantly, I open my eyes and tilt my chin down. My heartbeat stutters, and I stand, peering at my reflection in the water to get a better view.

While the lines I drew over him are squiggly and jagged, their path obviously an excuse for where I wanted to touch him, he has created a masterpiece. Detailed shells merge into beautiful arching curves of the sea. A sun, shrouded by wispy clouds, hovers over my right pectoral.

"You're making me look bad, Little Leaf," I say with a smile.

He stands before me, shifting from foot to foot and biting his lip in an all too tempting way. The marks on our bodies emit an ethereal glow between us.

"I like mine too," he says.

"Well, you should. It's also a masterpiece."

He shakes his head, auburn curls falling across his brow. "I mean, I had *you*. All you had to work on was *me*."

I don't know what happened to this man back in the Autumn Realm, but his self-talk needs improvement. I grasp his jaw and force his gaze to mine. "What are you talking about? You're beautiful."

He blinks as if he can't quite believe it, then clasps my wrist, this time not to push me away, but to hold me there.

"Is this where you take all your victims, thief?"

"Only the ones I really want to torment," I reply with a rueful grin. "Truthfully, I haven't brought anyone here before. It's a place I come when I need to get away from it all. To ground myself, I guess. Hadria's always full of people, noise, chaos...but no one else has found this little spot yet."

"Why me?"

"I mean, you're from Autumn. Not as if you'll be here long," I say quickly, but the real reason sits heavy in my gut. *Because I thought you'd like it.*

He steps away from me then and runs a hand through his hair. "You're right. The Autumn Realm awaits."

I force out a laugh and grab his arm. "But that's tomorrow's problem. Remember, there is one last thing I want to show you. We're still a long way from dawn."

# 4

# FARRON

I've seen more new and incredible things in one night than in the whole last decade of my life. But none are so incredible as the man sitting next to me. A mystery that, for once, I'm not rushing to uncover. *Who are you? Why are you showing me all these places? Does your heart nearly beat out of your chest when you look at me like when I look at you?*

For now, those questions can wait.

At least until the sun rises.

We sit on the morning-cold sand, toes buried deep. Around us, the Summer Realm begins to awaken. Farther down the beach, fishermen make their way to small skiffs. Bustling noises drift in from the city as the markets set up.

Soon, I'll have to find my way back to Soltide Keep and face all the consequences and judgment of my mother. The High Princess of Autumn and High Prince of Summer certainly wouldn't like me spending time with this ruffian. It would not be a match they'd approve of.

I sigh and lean forward over my knees, running a hand through my hair. What am I thinking? Match? I'm never going to see Day after tonight.

"Hey, look." Day's fingers brush the nape of my neck, and he draws my gaze upward.

The first hints of dawn paint the sky in delicate hues of pink and lavender. There's a crispness in the air, and the faint scent of salt and seaweed. Waves gently lap the shore.

"I don't want to return," I whisper.

"Then don't."

I turn and realize he's been watching me the entire time with that piercing turquoise gaze.

"Everyone has some idea of what my future is supposed to be," I say. "If I dare voice something different, it's met by closed ears."

"Tell me about it," Day says. "If anyone knew I was out here with *you*, then I'd be deader than a fish in a net."

"Really?" I say. "I can't imagine you letting anyone tell you what to do."

"If my family had their way, I'd be married off to a boring, snobby crybaby."

My stomach churns at the thought of him with someone else. Which is ridiculous. But when my fingers glided over his skin earlier, it was like I put a claim on him. The sun's rays peek above the horizon, making the faded blue lines on Day's chest appear golden. I could have touched him for a thousand years, memorized every muscle, every dip of hard flesh.

"Instead, you're out here with boring old me," I murmur.

"You're anything but boring, Fare." He tucks a strand of hair behind my ear. "I just want to exist in the moment, instead of being caught up in thoughts of the future."

"I've never been able to think like that."

"Why not start now?"

"It's not that simple." How can I explain that my decisions affect an entire realm? He'd never understand.

"Then start small. If you could do one thing right now, what would it be?"

I chew my lip and think. If I let go of the years and years of my future spreading out before me like an endless scroll of duties, what would I want in this moment?

I turn to look at Day, who is now gazing at the sea as if it holds all the answers he'll ever need. The rising sun casts a golden glow around him, haloing his figure with divine light. He belongs here, as if the sunrise has been painted for him.

His profile is sharp and striking, reminiscent of the statues in Soltide Keep. Strong jawline, high cheekbones, and eyes that hold a thousand untold stories. His hair, tousled by the sea breeze, catches the light, turning it to spun gold. He's beautiful, achingly so, in a way that feels otherworldly.

"I know what I want."

He lifts a brow, a smile curving on his lips. "And?"

My heart pounds in my chest, a wild, unsteady rhythm. I've always been cautious, measured in every action, but now, as I look at Day sitting there, bathed in the morning light, something in me breaks free.

Before I can second-guess myself, I close the distance between us. Day turns, his eyes meeting mine, wide with surprise. I grab his face in my hands, skin warm beneath my fingers. A slight tremor runs through him.

"Day," I whisper, my voice raw and trembling. And then, before he answers, I press my lips to his.

The kiss is soft at first, tentative, but then Day responds, his lips parting, and it deepens. A sensation of warmth and light and sweetness wafts over me, leaving me dizzy. Everything else falls away—the beach, the sunrise, the whole world—until there is only this, only us.

We pull apart, breathless and wide-eyed. There's a new glint in Day's gaze, something that mirrors the wild, unrestrained emotion I feel inside.

"Was that impulsive enough for you?" I grin. A storm swirls in his eyes, and for a moment, I wonder if I've made a terrible mistake. What if he *hated* that? "I'm sorry, I—"

"Fuck it," he growls.

Then he's on top of me, throwing us to the sand. His hand grips tight to my hair as he crashes his lips against mine. The kiss deepens, becoming something more urgent and consuming. Day grasps my shoulders as if to anchor himself. His touch burns, igniting a fire beside my heart that grows hotter and hotter.

We tumble, grains sticking to our skin, a tangle of limbs. He pulls me closer, and I can't get enough of him. His taste, his scent, the feel of his body pressed against mine. I never imagined it could feel like this.

I lift my hips as our bodies rub against each other. The deep moan in the back of his throat emboldens me further. My lips trail from his mouth to his jaw, along his neck. His skin tastes like salt and sunshine. His breath hitches again, and he arches into me, his hands roaming over my back, drawing me closer still.

My fingers glide across his body, mapping every inch, before resting against his heart. It beats wildly in the same cadence as my own.

Day's hips grind against mine, and I can feel his growing need. Our kisses become hungrier, more desperate, as if we can't get close enough, can't find enough ways to express the heat that's building between us.

I forget everything except salt and sunshine and *him*. I'm painted in the gold of his light, and I never want to leave. We roll in the sand until I'm above him.

He reaches up and brushes his knuckles along my cheek, and for someone with so much strength, the gesture is tender. "That's the perfect amount of impulsiveness, Little Leaf."

For once, I'm out of words and offer him what I can only imagine is an awkward smile, but he looks at me like I'm beautiful anyway. *He told me I'm beautiful.*

A noise snaps me out of the moment. Clattering footsteps, urgent and quick, approach from the distance. I narrow my gaze and see them along the docks. Autumn soldiers marching alongside Summer legionnaires. One of them stares in my direction, and my heart drops into my stomach.

I scramble to my feet, and Day follows. Sand clings to our bodies, the blue radiant essence smudged. The guards draw closer, eyes widening as they take me in.

"It's him!" one guard shouts, pointing at us.

"Oh fuck," Day swears under his breath.

"Don't tell me you actually are a thief?"

"Not exactly."

"Don't worry," I sigh, attempting to straighten the mess that is currently my toga. "They're here for me."

He laughs. "Not to say you aren't important, but I don't think they'd send this host for a wayward servant."

"Correct. They wouldn't." I give him one last look before I don a princely disposition and step protectively in front of him. "I never told you I was a servant."

Before he can respond, the first of the Autumn guards are upon us. "We've been searching all night for you, Prince Farron."

I sigh, unable to look back at Day.

But he, of course, breaks the silence. "Prince fucking *Fare*-on?"

Whirling, I don't see confusion on his face, only…anger. He storms up to one of the Summer legionnaires and grips him roughly by the shoulder.

"Listen here, Vitus," Day snarls, voice low with venom, "you and your little cronies will whisper no details of how you found me to the High Prince, or you can bet by low tide, I'll let everyone know about your escapade last full moon when you partook in too much honeyed wine."

"You can't assault a member of the royal guard!" I cry and grab Day's arm, but he easily shrugs me off.

The legionnaire's face blanches. He nods. "As you command, Prince Daytonales."

# 5

## DAYTON

The sun blazes high in the sky, casting a relentless heat over the realm. Even the goats have sought shade this morning. The pasture and old hut swim in my vision, and from halfway up Mount Tempitus, Hadria and the sea below look like nothing but a wavering mirage.

Sweat trickles down my back, soaking through my shirt. The scent of sunbaked earth and wildflowers fills my nose, mingling with the faint, musky smell of the goats grazing nearby.

I grip the hilts of my wooden swords tighter, the leather straps digging into my palms. Justus stands across from me, his weathered face calm and impassive as always, holding a wooden trident with the ease of someone who has wielded far deadlier weapons in the past. His eyes, sharp and knowing, see right through me, as if he's aware of the storm brewing inside.

"Focus, Dayton," Justus says. "Your mind is elsewhere."

The old fae poses as a reclusive goat herder, though there are whispers he was once an elite warrior in the ancient wars.

I can barely remember when or how I talked him into training me. I think it was my stubborn ass showing up day after day until he gave in. Sure, I could have many experts teach me at home, tutors in our own lavish grounds with brand new swords and shields.

But I'd take the old fae's rusty weapons and his audience of goats —who are actually quite judgmental—any day. There's something about Justus's lessons that pierces through my thick skull. Though probably not as much as he would like.

"Act, Dayton," Justus growls.

I grit my teeth and lunge forward. Justus deflects my blows with practiced ease. Every clash of wood against wood sends vibrations up my arms, but I press on, my movements fueled by the anger simmering inside me.

Fare. Or should I say Farron. Prince of the bloody Autumn Realm, and heir to its Blessing. I can't believe he *kissed* me. Can't believe without even a single drop of alcohol, I lost as much reason as if I'd drunk five pitchers of ale and threw myself at him. Threw myself so deep I was drowning—drowning in the crisp scent of his skin, the rich brown of his hair, the constellation of freckles over his nose.

Now, last night feels no better than a trap. I was a bug lured by sweet nectar only to be ensnared in a world of endless duty. Because that's what being a High Prince's consort would mean.

Kissing Fare is exactly what Damocles wanted. My older brother, always calculating, so certain of what's best for me. It's as if I played right into his hands, and I hate it. I despise feeling like a pawn in his grand schemes.

"Speak your troubles," Justus growls, "or clear your mind and focus."

"Damocles thinks he owns me," I roar with frustration then attack. "That he knows the best way to write my story."

"You are master of your fate, Daytonales," Justus quips, strands of graying hair falling across his brow.

"He wants to send me to Autumn, among the cold and death and dying!" The hot air burns my lungs, each breath a struggle. "To play consort to a prince."

"Then show him a path no other can chart but you."

My muscles ache, protesting the relentless pace, but I don't care. I need this—need to lose myself in the fight, to speak the words I only can find when swords are blazing.

I think Justus knows that. We're similar in that way.

"What if I already charted the course he wanted? What if I *liked* it?" I gasp. "Not the part of ruling, but the prince. We...we met. We kissed before I knew who he was."

Justus meets my fury with calm precision, his movements almost lazy in their efficiency. "Then you are still bending to Damocles's will."

The name of my brother fuels my anger further. I swing wildly, my vision narrowing to the points of my swords and the infuriatingly serene expression on Justus's face.

"I am not bending to his will!" I shout.

He sidesteps my next attack, his trident catching my blades and twisting them out of my grip. In an instant, I'm disarmed, and Justus is standing over me, the tip of his trident pressed against my chest.

"Enough." His gaze bores into mine. "You're not fighting me, Dayton. You're fighting yourself."

I slump to my knees, panting, the weight of his words hitting me harder than any blow. The anger seeps out.

"You can't let your brother's will control you," Justus continues, his voice gentler now. "You must forge your own path, make your own choices. Tell me, do you wish to see this Autumn Prince again?"

I close my eyes, the heat pressing down on me, and try to steady my breath. Farron's face flashes in my mind, and with it, a thousand conflicting emotions. Anger, desire, confusion. But beneath it all, something stronger. Something real. "Yes."

Justus kneels beside me, placing a hand on my shoulder. "You did not wish to court the Autumn Prince because you thought that path would bring you misery. But by denying yourself now, you are in misery."

I grind my teeth together. "You're right. You've given me an idea."

"Daytonales, why do I think you are not yet understanding my counsel?"

He only calls me by my full name when he thinks I'm being particularly annoying. I flash him a grin. "When have I ever done what I'm told?"

# 6

## FARRON

I pace back and forth across my guest room in Soltide Keep, unable to settle. My thoughts tumble too fast for my mind to make sense of them. Pathetic. Completely and utterly hopeless.

How could I let myself be caught in the Prince of Summer's undertow?

He hadn't been Daytonales last night. He'd been Day, effervescent and explosive. Trapped sunlight in the body of a mortal.

And I was stupid enough to think he'd have any interest in me.

*If my family had their way, I'd be married off to a boring, snobby crybaby.*

Daytonales hadn't seen me since I was a child, but that was enough for him to get a read on me. Even he, the brutish third son, knows I'm not cut out for anything. Especially not being High Prince.

With a groan, I collapse onto my bed, face down. The silken sheets are cool despite the scorching breeze that drifts in through the open balcony doors. How will I attend any of the other royal gatherings my mother and Damocles have planned for our two families? I can't imagine going to dinner, sitting across from Dayton as he winces, thinking how he'd kissed such a boring, snobby crybaby.

Ugh. This was all so much easier when he was the hideous toad who ruined my book.

"Hey! Fare?"

I jerk up. That voice…

"Hell-ooo? Come to the balcony!"

Day. It's Daytonales. It *has* to be. His voice seems to reverberate in the beat of my heart.

"I know you're up there! I saw you pacing a few minutes ago."

My body moves of its own volition, and I scramble out the doors, sliding across the marble floor of the balcony and catching myself on the railing.

Down below, Day stands on the rocks that separate the keep from the sea. Even from two stories up, I can still make out the intensity in his gaze.

A smile lights up his face when he sees me. "Fare."

I am helpless but to drink him in. I see why people say he's the spitting image of his eldest brother, Damocles. At first glance, the resemblance is obvious, and I could kick myself for not noticing it last night. But I was drunk on sea air and rebellion.

Now, I notice how different he is from his brother. There's a softness to him. Not in his body, which is all hard lines and cords of muscle, nor in his sharp jaw or straight brows. But in those eyes. Words from an old poet creep into my mind: *Tide-kissed, made of salt water and sea glass.*

A roguish grin appears on his face. "I knew you couldn't stay away from me."

Instantly, the haze of waxing poetic about his beauty drains away. That smile… What was once charming last night, now seems mocking. He's here to make fun of me. All the shame and humiliation I felt moments ago floods through me again.

"What are you doing here?" I snap.

He cocks his head. "Well, I didn't clamber over all these rocks at high tide just to stare at your balcony window." When I don't respond, he laughs. "I came to see you, of course."

"Well, I'm honored. The great prince of the arena deigns to visit the boring, snobby crybaby from Autumn. How kind of you! Now you've seen me, so you can go." With each biting word, I pray my red face isn't visible. I turn on my heels.

"Come on, Fare! Don't be like that!" he calls. "Didn't you have fun last night?"

Yes, I had fun. More fun than I've had in…in…in *ever*, if I'm being honest. But that's because it wasn't Farron running around Hadria. It was *Fare*. Fare, with no expectations, no responsibilities, no impending doom of ruling a realm. Of course, Fare is likable. Of course, Fare is fun.

"Go away," is all I manage before returning to my room. I duck to the side of the window and press my body against the wall so Daytonales can't spot me. Tears sting my eyes.

I count out ten breath cycles before I chance a peek back out on the balcony. Day's gone. *That was easy. Guess he didn't really want to see me.*

I turn around, debating if I should spend my afternoon lying face down on my bed or wading into the ocean until a sea hag puts me out of my misery, when I hear a grunting sound. Rushing closer to the railing, I look directly down to see Daytonales scaling the wall that leads to my balcony.

"Are you crazy?" I cry. "You could fall!"

Using the coral and shells encrusted on the side of the keep as hand- and footholds, Day flashes that grin at me. "This? This isn't crazy. This is madcap. Kooky, even. But we haven't stepped into crazy territory. Not even close."

"I'm not stepping into *any* territory with you, crazy or otherwise." I should run inside my room and lock the balcony doors. If he actually succeeds and doesn't fall and dash himself upon the rocks, I don't want to be here when he…when he…when he what?

What exactly is his plan?

"You're going to die," I call down to him.

Daytonales tests a patch of coral before heaving himself up to another handhold. His body glistens with oil, skin sunbaked. "People love to tell me that. Hasn't happened so far."

I lean on the railing and rest my chin on my hands. "Why do you want to see me so badly?"

"It's not *seeing* you that's eliciting this fanciful behavior. It's talking with you. Though, seeing you is a bonus." He winks and somehow appears as charming as ever despite hanging off the side of a building.

My heart gallops in my chest. *Settle down,* I inwardly snap at it. "Why do you want to talk to me? Me, who is boring and snobby and a crybaby?"

Daytonales rolls his eyes as he leaps for an upward patch of coral. Damn, he's scaling this wall fast. "Come on, Fare, I didn't mean it! We were *kids* when I thought that. I was an idiot."

"You're still an idiot, Daytonales."

"At least one of us has changed." Another sun-bright smile. "Call me Dayton. Call me Day. Call me *anything* but Daytonales. That's reserved for uptight nobles like my brother."

"Dayton..." He's so close to me now, I can see the sheen of sweat on his forehead, the tangles in his long hair.

He pulls himself up to the patch of coral beneath the railing, then stretches his hand upward. "What do you say, Farron? Give me a chance to make it up to you. Who knows, maybe you'll be a good influence on me, and I'll change too."

I could lock myself inside my room. Better yet, I could shove him off this wall. Now, *that* would be revenge for my ruined book years ago. But my heart has started that gallop again, and I can't seem to find the reins.

I reach down and clasp his arm. With a heave, I pull Dayton up over the railing. Though I must not recognize my own strength, for the force sends him careening into me. We tumble to the ground, him right on top of me.

"Hi." He smiles.

"Hi."

He doesn't make a move to get off of me. "So, you forgive me?"

"I suppose," I mumble. Mostly because I don't know what else to say when his lips are a breath away from mine.

"Perfect." He rolls, collapsing beside me. "So, I have a list of things to show you. Did you bring steel-lined shoes? Spring steel would be best, because this pond you *have* to see is beautiful, but the piranhas aren't so friendly—"

"You still want to hang out with me?"

Now, he's giving me a look like *I'm* crazy. "I climbed your whole balcony, didn't I?" He holds up his trembling hand. "Damn, I've never done that before. I could have died!"

"But what about your brother? I thought you didn't wish to give him the satisfaction of being right about, you know." My final word is an awkward mumble. *"Us."*

Dayton rolls onto his side. In a surprisingly delicate move, he strokes the edge of my face, pushing wayward strands of hair behind my ear. "You remember the saying, 'What they don't know, can't hurt them'?"

"Yes?"

Dayton grins. "Well, what Damocles doesn't know can't *help* him."

"So, we'll be, like, a secret?" I ask.

"Exactly."

Silence stretches before us until Dayton cups the back of my head and pulls me in. Our lips meet, his mouth commanding and gentle all at once. *Now I'm tide-kissed, too.*

Kissing Dayton back, all thoughts fade from my mind. All except one.

*What I know can hurt me.*

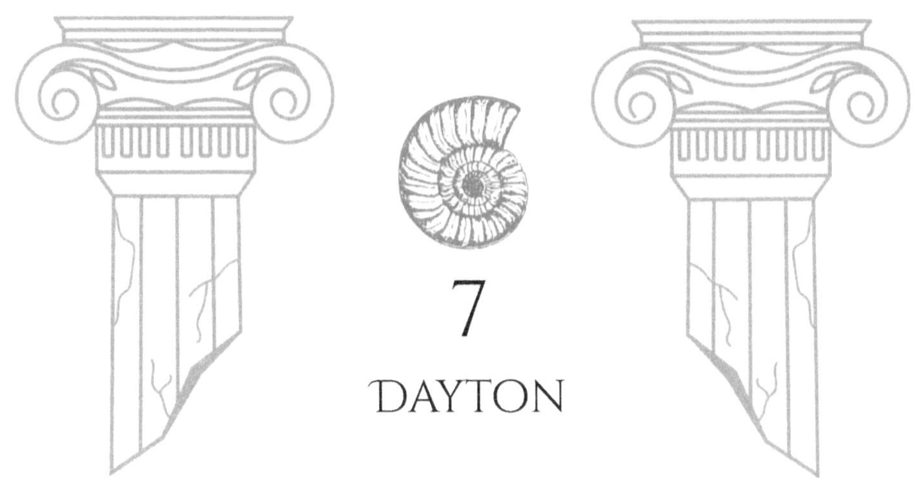

# 7

## DAYTON

Using a bush knife I "borrowed" from Justus's cottage, I hack through the thick vegetation. Judging by the light streaming through the thinning canopy, we've made it out of the deepest trenches of the jungle and are almost back to the coast.

Sweat drips down my spine. It's always warm in Summer, but the muggy heat within the forest is too much for even me to bear. Plus, I should have worn a shirt. I forgot how bad the mosquitos get in the bush.

But none of it bothers me. Not even a little bit. Not when Farron's walking beside me, grinning from ear to ear with pride from all the samples he collected.

It's been a couple weeks since his family arrived in Hadria, and we've spent every single day together. Soon enough, he'll return to the orchards and libraries of the Autumn Realm. Until then, I long to show him everything wonderful about Summer. Who knows? Maybe then he'll want to come back.

So far, I've taken him out on my skiff to sail the crystal-clear waters of the lagoon on the western coast. The local dolphins, pink as pigs and with permanent grins on their faces, love to chase the boats and will even swim beside you if you get into the water. Of course, I wasn't surprised to see  they took an immediate liking to Farron, twirling around him as soon as he jumped in. By the end of our afternoon, the creatures were taking turns whipping him around the ocean as he held onto their dorsal fins.

The next day, I'd shown him the peach orchards outside Hadria. There's a spring said to be blessed by our long-lost queen, and the water filters into the soil, causing the fruit to grow as large as a person's head. The creatures grow larger too, and dragonflies sail by, big as horses. But Farron, with his knowing eyes and quiet feet, crept up to them when they landed beside the trees and perfectly sketched one's eye, down to every facet. Of course, when I'd tried to approach, I'd sent the whole swarm erupting into the air. The good news was their wings tumbled a bunch of peaches down, and we practically waddled back to Hadria, full and sticky.

We've explored the markets and museums, beachcombed, and picnicked. We danced late into the night after stumbling upon a bonfire held by a nomadic band that sails the waterways on a skinny boat, making their living with song. We've laughed and talked and teased and kissed—kissed *a lot*.

And the best part is, Damocles has *no idea*. It hasn't even been hard. No one expects me to hang around the keep anyway, and I got my friend Claudius from the docks to pretend to be a professor from the university in need of an assistant with an out-of-realm perspective, which was an all too believable alibi for Farron.

My smile threatens to outmatch Farron's as I think of just how clever I am. If Damocles knew Farron and I were spending all this time together, that I was doing *exactly* what he and High Princess Niamh were scheming about for months, he would be insufferable. Damocles already feels like his every decision is blessed with wisdom from the Queen. And the worst part is, he's always right. Not most of the time. Not regularly. *Every single* decision Damocles has ever made has worked out for him and for Hadria. No wonder Mom made him High Prince. He's the perfect son of Summer, after all.

But I won't give him the satisfaction of knowing I don't think

Farron is a boring, snobby crybaby. To Dammy, it'd be another example of my poor judgment.

I'd much rather keep the Autumn Prince my little secret instead.

Farron bobs beside me, his auburn hair curling with the humidity, additional ribbons of freckles across his face which weren't there when he arrived in Summer. He's stripped off his fine tunic, so he's wearing a white undershirt that clings to his lean frame. Freckles even cover his shoulders and arms. *Summer looks good on you*, I think.

"I can't believe I found this." Farron reaches into his bag, pulling out a cranberry-red feather. "Nori's going to love it. But not as much as the snakeskin. To her, the creepier, the better."

Warmth tingles through my chest as I listen to the adoration in Farron's voice as he speaks of his family. "I wish I had a sister."

"It'd be nice for Nori, too. No other children in the royal families. It'd be great for her to have a friend to grow up with."

If my mother ends up having another child, they would be right around Nori's age. Farron's little sister has entered *serenage*, the time when fae aging slows. Fae babies grow quickly, similar to our human counterparts. I remember Mom explaining it to me as some sort of defense mechanism. By about school age, everything slows. Fae remain children for decades, and teenagers for even longer. A fae with wrinkles and hair of silver has seen centuries. Though I've never met one, some say there are still fae alive who once lived in the Above.

"Until then, I think Decimus is happy to play chaperone," I say, driving my knife down on a tall fern. "If Ma and Ovi have another baby, the three of us brothers would spoil them rotten."

As I push the broken fern away, bright sunlight streams through, and the crash of waves welcomes us. We step out of the jungle onto a grassy cliff, looking out over the turquoise ocean.

I flash Farron a grin. "Told you I'd find our way out of there."

"This doesn't look like where we came in." Farron turns in a circle, trying to get his bearings. "We didn't enter near the sea."

"Don't worry. I'll figure out where we are. I'll have you back home and tucked into bed with a cup of tea and a boring book before your sunset bedtime." As I give him a wink, he sticks his tongue out at me.

Seriously, though, I need to get my bearings. The last thing I want to do is get lost and embarrass myself in front of him. Quickly, I scan the horizon. It looks familiar. My eyes catch on a small sandy isle half a league offshore. There are four palm trees in a square, with the ones on the left and right bending toward the middle—

"Maybe we can pinpoint our location based on the coastal topography." Farron steps to the edge of the cliff.

I let out a strangled gasp and snatch Farron back by his undershirt.

"What's wrong?" he cries.

"I know where we are. This water is cursed."

"Cursed?" There's a teasing glint in Farron's gaze, but an underlying curiosity too.

I point to the isle, its outline clear against the cerulean sky. "See that? Legend has it Captain Katharine, the founder of Corsa Tuga, buried her most precious treasure on the isle and laid a curse on the water to protect it."

"What kind of curse?" Farron asks, his voice softer now, more serious. He takes a step closer, his shoulder brushing against mine. My heart flutters, but I keep my focus on the story.

"A monster lurks in the depths," I explain, unable to tear my eyes from his. "Even if you survive the hundred-foot jump into the ocean, don't get dashed upon the rocks, and can swim through the current, it doesn't matter. The creature will catch you."

Farron shudders slightly, but it's hard to tell if it's from fear or the closeness of our bodies. "What kind of creature?"

"Some say it's a kraken. Others claim it's the ghost of the captain herself," I continue, my voice low and steady. "But everyone agrees on one thing: no fae who has sought the treasure has returned."

"Have you ever tried?"

"No." I give a half laugh.

Farron raises a skeptical brow. "Jumping off cliffs into the ocean and tempting ghosts seems a very Dayton thing to do."

"Despite your preconceived notions of me, I'm not that brave. Or foolish."

Farron stays silent for a moment, then whispers, "Good. I don't want anything to happen to you."

The weight of his words hangs between us. The sunlight catches the strands of his hair, making them glow like embers.

"Farron," I start, but the words catch in my throat. Whatever this is, I need to stop it.

Farron's leaving Summer soon. He's heir to the throne of Autumn. And although he may not be a boring, snobby crybaby, one of my first impressions of him was correct.

Farron has a soft heart. I have no business holding onto something as fragile as that.

So, I laugh and slug him on the shoulder. "You're hilarious. I'm a *gladiator*. I face death every time I step onto the sands."

Farron's lip quivers, and he takes a long time answering. Then, he gives an awkward laugh and turns away from me. "I don't know. Maybe you need something to make you brave enough to face the curse."

"Like what?"

"Like a little push." He playfully shoves me, not hard enough to be serious, but enough to make me stagger.

"Oh, you want to take on a warrior of the arena?" I launch myself at him. We tumble onto the grass, laughing and wrestling. Whatever tension had hung between us drifts away into the breeze.

"The great Prince of Summer, afraid of ghost stories!" Farron teases, pinning me down before I twist and roll us over.

"I could take on a ghost!" I hold him down, our foreheads nearly touching. "I would face a ghost for you," I add, the words hardly louder than a breath.

His laughter fades. "You would?"

"Anything." My voice is barely a whisper, but in the stillness, it feels like a shout.

Before I can second-guess myself, I lean in, closing the distance between us. Our lips meet. The heat of the jungle pales compared to the fire igniting in my chest.

Farron's hand slides up to cup my face, pulling me closer as he deepens the kiss. All the noise in my head fades. Why does this keep happening? Every time I'm with Farron, it's like the haze in my mind clears. He burns away all the thoughts of what a disappointment I am, of how I can't trust my own judgment. There's only the blaze of his kiss and the swell of my heart.

I want more of him, more of this joy I get when I'm around him that drowns out everything else. My hand roams under his shirt.

"Day," he breathes, cheeks flushed.

I wonder if my weight is too much for him, and shift. The movement drags my pelvis over his, and I hold back a growl. He's hard. So fucking hard. Just like I am.

Can he feel me? Feel how fucking bad I want him? How hungry he makes me for every part of him?

Our kiss intensifies, becoming more desperate, and I think the answer to all my questions is *yes*.

His hands tangle in my hair, and I feel his heartbeat against my bare chest, matching the frantic pace of my own. I grind down on him, this need for closeness overwhelming.

His lips leave mine, trailing a path of fiery kisses along my jawline, down my neck. I gasp, fingers digging into his skin, urging him on.

With rough hands, I force his face back up, capturing his lips again. My tongue presses into his mouth, exploring, tasting. Lean muscles tense beneath my touch.

Finally, we break apart to catch our breath. Our cocks rub together, and I squeeze my eyes shut, so I don't lose control against him.

"I think you should get off me," Farron whispers.

I lean away, observing the same blaze in his eyes, the same overwhelming need. The realization that we're both so close to exploding is intoxicating.

Rolling off him, I force myself to stare at the sky, to come back to myself, even though it's the last thing I desire. I don't want to belong to myself. I want to belong to him.

But like taking on ghosts and cursed water, I'm nowhere near brave enough to do that.

"You're, uh, you're really good at this stuff," Farron mumbles, attempting to sound casual.

I chuckle and smirk at him. "Thanks. So are you."

"Well, I guess I have read a lot about it."

"Read about it?"

"Yeah, you know, in books and stuff. And those pamphlets the ladies hand out in the lower alleys of Coppershire. I mean, I don't go down there, but I found them in my tutor's briefcase once…" Farron suddenly seems very interested in a blade of grass.

Realization dawns on me, and I sit up, staring at him, agape. "Wait, Farron, have you never kissed anyone before?"

"I've kissed people!" he says. "I mean, a person. Okay, it was a wooden dummy but—"

"So, you're a virgin?"

His eyes go wide, and he opens his mouth to deny, but no words come out. His blush deepens to a sailor's favorite shade of night sky. "Um, maybe?"

I give a half-choked laugh. "You're 'maybe' a virgin? You can't exactly be unsure about that!" I collapse back to the ground.

"What? It's not like it's a big deal." He turns to stare at me.

I unsuccessfully attempt to suppress a groan and dig my palms into my eyes. "It's not a big deal normally. But you're the heir to the Autumn Realm, and I'm…I'm me." I look to the side, finding his golden gaze. "I don't want to ruin you, Fare."

He gives a sad smile. "It's not like I'm some delicate flower."

*That's just it, though.* He is like a precious rose, blooming toward the sun. And I'm the typhoon that will come in and uproot it.

With a sigh, I gather him in my arms.

"Maybe you need to jump," Farron murmurs.

"What?"

"To find the treasure on the isle. You've got to jump in the water feet first."

I pull him closer against me. "That's harder than it sounds, Little Leaf."

He smiles up at me, and there's something so earnest and genuine in that smile, it makes my heart ache. "I can be the push you need, if you want me to."

I don't reply; I just hold him. We lie there until the sun sets low on the horizon and the shadows of the palm trees on the isle lengthen across the water.

Farron doesn't understand. If I jump, it's not me who will get hurt.

It's him.

# 8

# FARRON

I've returned to my favorite spot in the ballroom of Soltide Keep with the usual company: the marble busts. Poor Aeneas has been repaired, his shards held together with gold filament. Not to defend my clumsiness, but I can't help thinking it makes him even more beautiful.

The Farewell Gala is in full swing, lively music filtering through the ballroom, rich food served on platters, and my family getting in their last bits of mingling before we depart. Tomorrow morning, we'll be on the road to Coppershire. The weeks spent in Summer, filled with late-night rendezvous, sights I'd only read about, and kisses that sent my mind spiraling, will become nothing but a memory. A memory that will fade, as the bright green leaves of summer fade to withered husks in autumn.

I feel a tug at my tunic and spin, but there's no one there. There's a pull on my other side and a little giggle. I look over my other shoulder, but again, there's no one, though I spot a patch of reddish-brown hair poking out from behind Aeneas's bust. Not in the mood to play, I lunge forward, snatching my brothers, Dom and Billy, from their hiding place.

"Go find someone else to bother," I growl.

"Aw, you're no fun tonight." Dom shoves his hands in his pockets. The twins would be identical if not for the differences in the spattering of freckles dusted across their faces.

Billy kicks the base of Aeneas's bust, sending him wobbling again. "Yeah, you're all mopey."

I steady the statue and glare at them. "Sorry, I don't feel like being the target for your pranks."

Dom nudges his twin. "I found a crab down on the beach. Let's go sneak it into the big one's pocket." They skuttle off across the ballroom toward Damocles.

I sigh, digging my hands in my pockets, not caring how much of a child I must look. My brothers are right. I *am* grumpy.

I don't know how to fake a smile when my heart feels as if it's breaking.

It's not only that we're leaving tomorrow, my moments with Dayton falling away like leaves upon the wind. It's that I'm leaving like *this*.

Dayton's leaning against a wall toward the back of the ballroom, the full moon's light shining through and basking his face in its milky glow. I've known his exact location since the ball started, known what he's had to drink and eat, what songs he's danced to, and who he's spoken to, because I haven't been able to take my eyes off him once.

And I know he hasn't looked my way.

Because I don't exist to Dayton when our families are around. He'll roughhouse with my brothers, listen to my sister's rambling, spar with my father, debate with my mother, but I could be a ghost to him. A story as unbelievable as Captain Katharine's creature.

Not that Dayton's lacking for company. Right now, a gaggle of women surround him, fluttering their eyelashes and stroking his arm at every opportunity. Dayton's got that curved grin on his face that I can't stand. The charming, roguish, oh-so-fake smile.

Maybe I'm the idiot for thinking the one he'd been giving me all these weeks wasn't fake, too.

The only person at this party who appears to be more miserable than me is Damocles. So, Dayton got his way. His big brother and my mother won't have the satisfaction of running yet another aspect of our lives.

We made this decision together, didn't we?

So why do I feel so out of control?

My hands tremble, and my breathing becomes so rapid that I struggle to catch my breath. How am I to return home like this, in this state of misery? Never knowing which part of Dayton was the truth: the one that stares at me with stars in his eyes when we're alone, or the one who treats me like a plague boil in front of our families.

Maybe all the days we spent together meant nothing to him, but they meant a lot to me. Dayton *did* something to me. Stoked the embers within my heart until they were desperate for kindling. And if I don't figure out what I mean to Dayton, those embers are going to burn me from the inside out.

Hands clenched into fists, I search the ballroom until I see the second-born Prince of Summer, Decimus. He's at the buffet table, filling a plate with olives and figs. I speed walk out onto the dance floor, narrowly avoiding being swept into a twirl by one of the guests.

"Decimus," I say as I approach, voice surprisingly steady.

"Farron!" Decimus holds out his plate. "Fig?"

"No, thank you. Can you give your brother a message from me?"

Decimus lowers his plate to the table and turns to face me head-on. He's taller than me, heavily muscled from years in the arena. A rippled scar runs across his collarbone. Kindness flashes in his dark brown eyes. "Dayton?"

I don't know how he knows I meant Dayton and not Damocles, but I nod. I need to get the words out now before I lose my nerve. "Tell Dayton…I'm ready to jump, and I'm not afraid of the water. The treasure awaits, and he gave me the push I needed."

Decimus raises a brow. "What?"

"Tell him exactly that! Either he'll understand or he won't." I turn away from him and walk as fast as I can to the door. My heart beats in a terrified rhythm, but I need to do this.

By the end of the night, either I'll understand…or I won't.

# 9

## DAYTON

Breath comes ragged from my throat as I sprint through the bush, bare feet flying over rocks and twigs.

What in the fucking stars is he thinking?

He couldn't. He wouldn't…

But that's just it. I don't *know* Farron. We've spent every day together for the last month, but I still don't know him. Because every time he got a little too close, I pushed him away. With averted gazes, snide comments, or a new person on my arm, I pushed him.

Pushed him straight over the edge.

For what? I can't remember a single conversation I had with anyone tonight, but I can remember every word he's ever said.

My hair flies in a tangled halo as I break out of the jungle and onto the cliff. The wind whips at my bare chest, at the thin piece of purple fabric I wear around my hips. My legs burn hot, my lungs hotter. I don't think I've run so fast in my life.

How long ago had Farron left the party? When Decimus strutted up to me and passed on his message, I'd asked when Farron had departed. Decimus had shrugged, saying he couldn't recall. He'd gotten caught up in a jig with Paddy before he remembered to tell me.

I stagger in a circle, searching the cliff, only the light of the full moon to guide me. What had he meant, *I'm ready to jump*? Surely, he could only be talking about Captain Katharine's Isle.

He can't be serious about jumping. I'll find him standing on the cliff, the whole thing a cruel joke. Then I'm going to punch him so damn hard for making me run all the way here. Only Justus can get me to push myself like this.

Just as I've convinced myself there's no actual way Farron intends to jump into the cursed waters, I catch sight of a silhouette on the edge of the cliff.

Tall, lean body, shirtless, wearing only a pair of breeches. A wild thatch of hair blows in the wind.

"Farron," I breathe. I *knew* he wouldn't actually—

The silhouette looks up at the moon, chest rising and falling. In the frosted glow, I see the shine of his eyes.

Farron steps off the edge.

*"Farron!"* I scream. Sprinting harder than I ever have before, I make it to the edge of the cliff, fling myself to my knees, and peer into the dark.

Down below, white waves crash on the rocks. There's no sign of the Autumn Prince.

My body reacts as if it doesn't even have to wait for my mind. Every part of me knows what I need to do.

Taking a deep breath, I jump from the cliff and descend toward the cursed waters below.

The wind howls in my ears. There's nothing but air on all sides of me. My stomach shoots up into my throat. I've cliff jumped hundreds of times before, but never this high. Never without checking the waters below. I try to make sense of every-thing as I plummet, the waves rushing up to meet me. There are so many rocks—did Farron hit one on the way down? Will *I* hit one?

Fear claws at my throat as the spray of the churning water strikes my skin. I brace for impact.

I slam into the water with a violent splash. My bones ache with the impact, but I'm not dashed against the rock. I'm swept up in cold darkness, the current tugging at me from each direction. I fight the pull, trying to orient myself.

Breaking through the surface, I gasp for breath. A wave sweeps over my head, and I'm forced to fight for air again. I only get a moment above water before a swell pulls me under, but I keep trying.

"Farron!" I yell each time I'm able to get a lungful of air. Where is he? Is he alive? Is his body shattered on the rocks?

Moonlight shimmers off the isle, about half a league away. If he survived the fall, he'd swim there.

*This water is cursed,* a childish part of my mind says.

Sputtering against the waves, I growl, "Fuck it."

Curse or not, I'll find Farron.

Arm over arm, I cut through the water, the moon my lifeline. I can do this. I've swum through rougher waters. One arm in front of the other—

A force slams into me, and I'm sent tumbling down into the dark. I right myself, eyes fighting through the ocean. Did Farron find me? What else could have—

A shape materializes. Four powerful legs made of currents of water. Muscular body rippling like waves. Eyes shining with malevolent moonlight. A monstrous horse made entirely of the sea surges forward. Its liquid form shifts and flows as it canters toward me.

I gasp and try to swim for the surface. The creature gets to me first. The horse rears up, then strikes. Its hooves, solid despite their liquid appearance, pound into my chest, driving the last breath from my lungs.

I claw at the water, trying to find purchase, but the horse doesn't stop. It pushes me further and further down. My ears pop and my lungs burn. A spell, there's a spell for breathing underwater. I try to summon my magic, but I can't get a hold of it. Mom is always telling me to put down my swords and practice the ancient powers. Why didn't I listen to her?

I beat at the horse's legs but it's no good, my movements too slow in the water. The horse sneers, an angry expression, filled with hate. Is this Captain Katharine's curse or just another scared beast like me?

My vision blurs. The weight of the water pushes against me on all sides. I'm drowning. A Prince of Summer, *drowning*.

What a waste. Just like Damocles always thought.

Though, if I have to go like this…chasing after Farron…

At least I'm dying for something worthwhile.

Golden light shimmers through my vision. Is this it? Death? Will the Orb of Ancestors still take my spirit, or will I be denied that honor because I didn't die upon the sands?

This gold light of death sure is beautiful though. It appears above us. Even the horse seems distracted by it, looking up, the pressure of its hooves releasing.

*Hey, this is* my *death. Let me have it,* I think to the horse.

The gold light shifts, and I see it's the outline of a person. A man.

One with a thatch of wild hair.

*Farron.*

I'm not dying, at least not yet. But Farron is lit up like one of those glowing orbs always floating around Keep Oakheart. And he's got the horse's full attention.

*No, Fare, no. You've got to run…*

The horse kicks away from me, trotting over to Farron. Farron lays his golden hands upon the beast's neck. Slowly, he lowers his head, brow to brow with the horse. The creature's moonlit eyes close.

I blink, unsure if my vision is too darkened to understand what I'm witnessing. The creature nuzzles Farron's neck, then kicks through the dark water, looking playful. Like a foal. With one look back at me, a snort of bubbles erupts from its nostrils, and it darts off into the water, disappearing as if it were never here at all.

I shake my head. Farron, a siren in his own right, charming dolphins and dragonflies and cursed horses. Charming those beasts as he charmed me.

Farron wraps his arms around my waist and kicks. Something deep within me finds strength, and I kick, too. In moments, we break through the water. It's calm, the surface like glass.

"Are you an idiot?" Farron cries. His golden glow fades, and now he's wreathed in white moonlight. "Why did you jump?"

"I pushed you, you pushed me," I say, voice hoarse.

Farron shakes his head then laughs. "I didn't think you'd follow me."

"Yeah, well"—I lace one arm around his back, the other through his hair—"apparently the boy I've taken to is *crazy*."

A grin creeps up his face. "That wasn't crazy. Madcap, maybe. Kooky, even. But you haven't seen crazy. Not yet."

Farron kisses me, lips of salt and sea. An Autumn boy tasting of Summer.

A taste I would drown for all over again.

Finally, we pull away, gasping. I look to the isle. "We made it this far."

"Let's go get our treasure," Farron says.

I don't respond, only capable of nodding.

Because damn if I haven't already found mine.

# IO

## FARRON

"**I** knew it!" Dayton cries. Sand sticks to his skin, still wet with ocean water, and moonlight paints him in shimmering strokes. He's positioned in the center of Captain Katharine's Isle, right in the middle of a square formed by four palm trees. "I told you it'd be here."

"You told me," I murmur. I'm lying against one of the trees, still marveling at the turn of events. The gentle roar of the waves is the only sound that accompanies us, a soothing rhythm that mirrors the steady beat of my heart. This has to be the strangest—and most wonderful—night of my life. Never did I think I'd end up off the coast of Hadria on a supposedly cursed isle with the Prince of Summer. And that he'd be looking at me with those turquoise eyes so filled with joy, especially after I almost got him killed.

I still don't know what came over me. Walking to the coastline. Staring into the abyss, drawn to the dark depths. Feeling like if I was losing Dayton, I could at least feel a sense of him within the sea.

But he'd followed me. Followed me all the way off the edge.

These waters, supposedly cursed by Captain Katharine, were none other than the territory of a kelpie. They're common inhabitants in the lochs and rivers of Autumn; this one must have lost its way in the waterways between our two realms. No wonder it was so scared and angry. I'd been able to calm the beast and let it take in my scent. Hopefully that will be enough for it to find the path back to Autumn.

Dayton looks handsome beyond comprehension. His long hair is slightly wavy with dried saltwater, his skin caked in sand. Most beautiful of all is that delighted smile on his face. He should be *furious* at me for jumping in. For risking my life and his. But when we reached the shore, the only thing he wanted to do was start looking for the treasure.

Now, he reaches down into the hole he's dug, tugging out a wooden chest.

I walk over and crouch beside him. "Captain Katharine's treasure," I breathe. "It's real."

"Of course, it's real! You need to have more faith," Dayton says, a victorious grin on his face.

I keep my eyes on him, instead of the treasure. "Maybe I do."

With an easy yank, Dayton breaks the rusty lock. "Ready?"

"Ready."

Our fingers brush as we both grasp the lid. It creaks in protest, revealing...

"Sand," Dayton whispers. "Captain Katharine's treasure is *sand?*"

Inside, there's a mound of red dust. I reach within, sifting the grains through my fingers. They're fine and velvety. Perhaps once, they were something more, the ashes of a forgotten world. But now, they're nothing but dirt in a rotting box.

Disappointment is clear in Dayton's expression. "All these years, I pictured what it could be. Jewels and gems, mythical weapons, or maps to hidden cities. I guess none of the stories were real. It's just sand."

"Maybe not," I say. "Let me try something."

I pick up a large handful, holding it tight between my palms. Warmth radiates from my chest down into my fingertips. I prefer written spells to help channel my magic, but burning...burning I know how to do.

Especially around Dayton.

The red sand begins to coalesce, grains fusing together with the heat.

"Quickly," I whisper. "We need to cool it."

Dayton raises a brow, then covers my hands with his. A stream of cold water pours from his palms. Steam rises from our clasped grip, a symphony of fire and water. Our power seems to meet where our skin touches. I think of the legends in Autumn, of magic weaving together. It feels like that now, our individual powers braiding into something more.

The steam ebbs out, and Dayton pulls away from me. I open my palms, revealing a piece of red sea glass, smooth and luminous.

A smile tugs at the edge of Dayton's lip as he takes the sea glass and holds it up to the moonlight. "We made this together," he whispers.

"Something to remember me by, when I go back to Autumn."

Dayton clasps the sea glass tight in his palm, then tucks it into a fold of the purple wrap around his waist. "I'll never be able to forget you, Fare. Trust me."

My throat tightens. I don't want to become a memory to Dayton. To be nothing but fading conversations, a face once clear that becomes foggy over time. Doesn't he understand this is so much more than political alliance or family scheming? Whatever this is between us is so real, I feel like I could touch it. I *need* to touch it.

I trail a hand across Dayton's sandy cheek before clasping his neck. "I barely remember who I was when I first came here. You've changed me, Day. I can't go back to who I was before you."

"Fare—"

I can't let him speak. Because he'll tell me to stop being ridiculous. That I've fallen too hard, too fast for him. Instead, I pull his lips to mine. So what if this is what Summer's made me? Ridiculous. Down in the muck of this thing…whatever it is. Need. Obsession.

Love.

Dayton kisses me back. Hard. His hands wrap around my body, fingers so rough, I imagine bruises forming on my skin. His handprints, marring me. I wish they were brands, claiming me as his forever. Our kiss grows more frantic, my fingers gripping his hair. It feels like we're fighting with our lips, a battle we're both too afraid to wage with words.

"Fuck, Farron," Dayton growls against my mouth. He grabs my ass and thrusts his pelvis against me. His iron-stiff arousal sends my pulse skittering. I can't stop moving; I have to keep kissing him, have to keep roaming my hands across his skin. If any of this stops, he might suggest going back to the keep. The keep with all those judging eyes that force us apart. Then, tomorrow, I'll be gone.

A fading memory.

I push firmly on Dayton's chest, guiding him down to the sand. He tugs me with him, and I land on top of his solid body, never tearing my mouth from his lips. His cock feels hard as steel, pressing against my abdomen. My own presses painfully against my breeches. Shifting positions, I jut forward so he can feel my arousal against his. He pulls away from my kiss to groan, the sound part curse, part my name, and part unintelligible blather.

Pride swells in my chest. He isn't so infallible after all.

I go to capture Dayton's mouth again, but he grabs the side of my head and holds me at a distance. His gaze is so intense.

"Farron," he says lowly, "I want to do right by you. You know that, don't you?"

"Of course," I say. He doesn't know that he could ask me to crawl behind him and I would consider it a privilege.

Dayton pushes the hair back from my eyes. "I will never ask you to do anything you're uncomfortable with."

"I want this," I breathe.

"But you've never... I'm not exactly the kind of person I'd choose for my first time."

Turning my face to kiss his hand, I murmur, "Well, I guess I'm smarter than you."

Dayton barks a laugh before his gaze softens. "You sure about this, Little Leaf?"

"I've never been sure about anything in my life. But I'm sure about this. About you."

"Here?"

"Here," I breathe. "Anywhere. Any time. Any weather. Any season. As long as you're you."

Dayton brushes tears from my cheeks that I hadn't realized were falling. "A deal. I promise to always be me. And you've got to promise me you'll always be you, okay?"

"It's a promise," I whisper.

The smile that crosses Dayton's face is so beautiful, I swear it could rival the sun. He pulls me flat to his chest, caging me in with his arms, and simply holds me. I close my eyes, feeling the strong beat of his heart.

After a moment, I look up at him. His gaze has shifted from its softness. There's a hunger there that makes my stomach flip.

Dayton pushes me to the sand, so I land on my back. Then he clambers over me, running his rough and calloused fingers along my chest. With my body pinned by his muscular legs, I'm completely at his mercy.

He's going to touch me. He'll reach down and grab my cock. I can picture it now, his huge hands wrapped around my length, handling me with aggressive strokes.

But he doesn't. Minute after minute passes with him only rubbing my chest. He flicks a tongue over his lips, and I notice his gaze has shifted again, his moods as changeable as the wind.

Is he...nervous? Nervous to touch me?

Perhaps he thinks I'm fragile, an Autumn leaf easily crumbled. I'll show him how much I've changed since that first night.

I reach underneath the folds of his purple wrap and grasp the base of his cock.

Dayton arches his back and pushes into my grip. I tug on the knot tying the wrap together and pull the cloth free, tossing it to the ground. Dayton springs loose in all his glory, his lower abdomen rippling with muscle, a line of blond hair trailing from his belly button. The sides of his ass are carved like marble.

And his *cock*.

Freed from the fabric, it erupts forth, thick and hard. It curves upward, the tip glistening in the moonlight. Blood rushes in my ears, and I have to remind myself to breathe. A million ideas burst inside my head, all the desire I've fought down these last few weeks. But he's right in front of me, his cock as beautiful as he is.

It's as if freeing Dayton of his clothes has reawakened him. He grabs my hand and directs it to the base of his cock, then covers my fingers with his. Together, we move over his length, stroking up and down. I feel myself panting, heart near breaking through my ribs. I want to know what Dayton's expression is, but I can't tear my gaze away from the titanic erection in front of me.

"Fuck," Dayton growls, increasing our speed. "I love the feel of your hand, Fare."

Finally, I shift my eyes upward to hold his gaze. His turquoise eyes shimmer. "Let me," I beg.

He nods and pulls his hand away. Now, I clasp his cock with both my palms, one stacked on top of the other, and start a rhythm. Up and down, each action eliciting a shiver or moan from Dayton. The weight of his body on my hips and the look of pleasure on his face make my cock surge with blood. I grit my teeth, moving faster, wanting to give him more and more—

I drop his length and sit up on my elbows. Dayton smiles down at me, expression almost drunk. "Wrists hurt?"

"No." My gaze darts back to his pulsing member, the pearl of moisture on the tip. "I want to try something."

"We don't have to move so fast—"

I push on his chest, guiding him off me and onto the sand. He lies on his back, gaze questioning. "Trust me, Dayton. Can you trust me?"

"Of course," he breathes.

I kiss him softly on the lips, then work my way down, along his jaw, the thick cords of his neck, his collarbone, over his muscular pectorals. I lick my way along the ridges of his abdomen, tasting dried saltwater. When I get to his hip bones, I suck in a deep breath. His body tenses.

I've never felt this before—this intense, sickening yearning. Before, I thought this kind of desire was saved for fairy tales. Or maybe it only existed for people with mate bonds, that rare, inescapable love that's descended from the stars.

But that's how I feel now: possessed. As though, if I don't have a part of my skin against his skin, I might go mad with longing.

Slowly, I kiss the base of his cock. It's so close, I'm a bit intimidated by its length and girth. But I'll take my time. It seems like I've been waiting forever.

Flicking my tongue out, I lick up and down. Like his torso, it's hard and tastes of salt.

Dayton groans. Encouraged, my tongue sweeps in longer strokes before swirling around his tip. With a greedy motion, I suck the head into my hollowed cheeks. His hips jerk upward, slamming his cock into the back of my throat. I gag, but don't let go.

With one hand, I cup his heavy balls. They're flushed with color, and I run a soft finger down the seam.

He jerks a hand out, weaving his fingers through my hair. "Gods, Farron, you're so good at this."

I don't stop my motion, but my mind races. Am I actually good or is he just saying that? Surely, Dayton has had a plethora of partners, ones who might have even studied the art of pleasure. Here I am, having done nothing but reviewed some pictures from books at the back of the library—

I stop myself. No, I won't let my self-doubt get to me. Not when every part of me is screaming how *right* this is. How my lips belong on him, how he belongs in me. I know how to pleasure him, as if the instructions were written on my heart.

With one hand on his balls, the other stroking his shaft, and my mouth around the tip, I work Dayton until he's quivering and moaning underneath me. His fingers dig trenches into the sand. Deeper and deeper, I try to take him, my pace increasing—

"Okay." Dayton sits up, pushing me off his cock with a wet *pop*. His face is flushed, and he's starry-eyed, as if having awoken from a dream.

"Everything okay?" I ask. "Did I do something wrong?"

"The opposite." He grabs my chin and drags me up for a kiss. "I want more of you."

My pulse skitters, and all I can manage is a nod.

"But first," Dayton says, guiding me to my back, "there's something you have to know about me. I never let my lovers come only once."

He wants me to know this about him. Because he thinks we'll do this again? I have to fight to keep the embarrassing smile off my face.

"First, these need to go." Dayton grabs the waistband of my breeches. "Wearing pants to a Summer gala? *Tsk tsk.* Even your father was wearing traditional Summer garb."

"I tried the wrap skirt. Too breezy," I mumble.

"Afraid I might see something?" Dayton smirks. "May I?"

I nod. Dayton pulls on my waistband and yanks my breeches straight off my feet, tossing them to the side. My cock, hard to the point of pain, flings free.

Dayton's eyes roam over me, from my toes, curling and uncurling in the sand, up my lean legs, to settle on my cock. He licks his lips. Somehow, his gaze seems even more intimate than any touch.

"You are glorious," he murmurs.

Although I've never felt a love for weaponry, it is part of being a Prince of Autumn to train. I have always fancied the art of a duel, the satisfaction of the ache in muscles after training. I've also taken to long runs through the hillside, where my mind can wander far away from reality. Though I'm not heavily muscled like Dayton or his brothers, the outlines of my muscles are clear beneath my freckled skin.

I've never liked being on display for anyone. But I'd lie here forever if Dayton wanted me to.

"I'm going to make you feel like you've never felt before," Dayton says. He lowers between my legs, then lifts my thighs up onto his shoulders, so my lower back is off the sand. I gasp at the sudden vulnerability of it—not just my cock on display, but my ass, too.

His tongue snakes out and begins to lap at my cock, running the length of my balls up to the tip of my head. I cry out, unable to stop myself. He's right; I've never felt anything like this before. His mouth is wet and warm, and every inch of skin that he caresses comes alive. My heart feels like it may burst into flames.

His hands massage my thighs, soft and gentle, but his pace gets more demanding, sucking me deep into his throat. Need pulses through me.

With greedy gulps, he sucks my balls into his mouth, one then the other. Then his lips wander lower, kissing the skin beneath, then lower…

I suck in a breath.

"Relax," Dayton murmurs against my skin. "I'll look after you."

All I can do is surrender to his expert touch. I look up at the sky, swirling with stars, and let myself feel the sensation. Dayton's warm breath against my entrance, then a string of soft kisses that evolves into the lap of his tongue. All thoughts fly from my mind and there is nothing but the soft caress of his mouth and the burning hot need in my cock.

"I'll look after you," Dayton says again. He slips my legs from over his shoulders. My eyes widen as I watch him spit onto two fingers then rub his saliva on my hole. There's an expression of reverence in his stare. "If it's too much, you tell me to stop, okay?"

"Okay," I breathe.

One of his hands grips my cock. The other trails down to my ass. With synchronized movement, he strokes my length and plunges a finger inside of me.

Stars erupt in my vision, and I gasp out. I barely have time to comprehend the intensity when Dayton begins his rhythm. Up and down, in and out. My entire body shoots with electricity, like a lone tree in a lightning storm. His name tumbles from my lips over and over again.

"I'm going to give you more now," he grunts, and I see his own erection is harder than ever. "Two fingers. Is that okay?"

"Yes," I cry. "Yes, yes, Dayton."

My body responds for him, relaxing and opening. In a single movement, Dayton plunges two fingers within me. Nothing has ever felt as good as this. I buck against his hand, wanting more of him in me, on me. Dayton grits his teeth and strokes my cock faster. I'm like his dual swords, and he wields me perfectly.

My vision is a scattering of night sky and stars, but I catch his gaze. He holds my stare, and I can't help myself anymore. Desire and pleasure and pure joy erupt through me. His hands all over me are too good.

"Dayton, I have to—"

"Come for me, handsome. Come for me." Dayton moves swiftly, leaning down and capturing me in his mouth. The warm pressure of his tongue, combined with the rhythm of his hands, is too much for me to bear. I squeeze my eyes shut, and lights skitter through the darkness. My body trembles over and over, and it feels like my whole chest has burst into the blaze that started in my heart. Dayton gulps, greedily sucking up every drop of my pleasure.

I lie, quivering, vision clearing into the night sky. Dayton releases his hold on me, then scoots to my side. He's got the proudest grin I've ever seen.

"You taste amazing," he says.

"Show me," I murmur.

He leans down, embracing me with an open-mouth kiss. The soft roar of the waves against the beach, the warm air, the rich smell of palm trees and briny water, and now the crash of his mouth on mine fill my head with an intoxicating rush.

I know what comes next. I imagined losing my virginity countless times. In my visions, there was always a bed, and usually a pretty, soft-spoken woman. Nothing could be more different than this moonlit beach, with this brash, loud gladiator who laughs too much and reads too little. Yet, I could not imagine anything more perfect.

Dayton sits up and moves between my legs. Just staring at his form is enough to return my cock to attention.

"Have I ever told you how happy I am you tried to escape out that window?" he asks, absently trailing a hand across my body.

"Hey, I didn't *try* to escape. I did, despite being hindered by a thief."

Dayton laughs and rolls his eyes exaggeratedly. "I didn't steal anything."

*Oh, but you did. You stole my sense, my reason, the very breath from my lungs. You stole the peace from my soul and every thought that dared not be of you.*

"Why are you looking at me like that?" Dayton whispers.

I don't know how I'm looking at him, so I give my head a shake, forcing on a normal smile. "You stole my time in Summer, and I'll forever be glad of it."

Dayton lowers his body over mine, guiding my legs on either side of his hips, and positioning his cock at my entrance. "It's mine forever now."

"Forever," I whisper.

"You tell me to stop, and I stop, okay?" Dayton says, face serious.

I nod, and Dayton cups the side of my face. "Beautiful." Then, holding himself up by his arms, he pushes into me.

My breath hitches, and my eyes flutter shut. Pain shoots through me as Dayton thrusts inch by inch. I suck in a deep breath, willing my body to relax. Currents of pleasure begin to stream in, a river mixing with the ocean of tension. But when I open my eyes to meet Dayton's gaze, euphoria floods through me. We're moving together, our bodies like one. All this distance I've felt from him these weeks, all the fear, disappears with each stroke.

Every thrust sends tremors through my body, sharp jolts of sensation cutting through the heat and desire. Dayton's breathing quickens, and I match him. Everything we do is in sync, in rhythm. Two shards of sea glass, the broken pieces fitting perfectly together.

The slap of our bodies rings out over the crash of waves. Dayton's touch becomes rougher, his movements more urgent. His gaze burns with rare intensity. I can see the animalistic hunger in him, the hunger for me. It's intoxicating.

"Fuck, Farron," he growls. "You're perfect."

*Perfect for you?* What else could I ask for? With Dayton, I feel the courage of a lion. Maybe I could be High Prince if he were by my side. We could rule together, spending our days serving Autumn and our nights serving each other.

The thought heightens my desire. A strangled cry escapes me, and Dayton reaches down, fevered, and grabs my cock, stroking again to match the rhythm. Stuffed full inside, my cock clenched in his grip, the wave of my passion begins to crest.

"Dayton, I-I need to—"

"Fuck, yes, Farron. I'm going to come with you, okay? You come and I'll come. I'll fill you up. Okay?"

His words are urgent, needy. I can't keep it in anymore. The orgasm crashes over me as the ocean did when I leapt from the rocks. It feels like falling. My cock twitches and erupts across my chest. Dayton roars out, shoving deeper than ever before. My eyes nearly roll back into my head as I'm filled beyond what I thought possible.

The world dissolves into a haze. Dayton collapses on top of me, his weight calming. He murmurs unintelligible words between kisses on my neck. I stroke his wavy hair and stare up at the stars. Which one did he come from? Which one did I? *Why does it feel like we came from the same one?*

We lie there like that for what could be minutes or hours. Finally, Dayton groans and rolls off me, erupting into joyous laughter for no reason at all, and I can't help but join in. Then he stands, scoops me over his shoulder, and carries me into the surf.

After we wash, we collapse back down on the small grassy patch around the palm tree, both staring up into the sky.

Dayton entwines our fingers. "I don't want you to leave tomorrow."

My breath catches. "Me neither."

"There're so many other places we could do this! There are thousands of isles in Summer. We should make it our goal to do this on all of them." He rolls over and gives me a wild grin.

Now, my breathing quickens. He wants to keep doing this with me. He doesn't want me to leave.

I knew it. I knew Dayton felt the same way.

Facing him, I gently run my hand along his cheek. "Let's do it. A thousand places. Even if it takes us forever."

Dayton laughs. "Forever is a very long time."

The words I want to say feel too big for this little island, so I smile and stare into his turquoise eyes.

*Forever isn't long enough if I'm with you.*

# II

## DAYTON

The Autumn nobles are readying to depart. The vibrant colors of their carriages contrast sharply against the pale landscape of Soltide Keep. I stand near the edge of the courtyard, my heart a tangle of emotions, watching as Farron and his people ready themselves for the journey home.

Damocles stands with Niamh, clutching her hands as they engage in some last-minute gossip—no doubt lamenting that they couldn't get a formal engagement out of Farron and me. In fact, as far as Damocles is concerned, we're barely amicable acquaintances.

I certainly don't make my acquaintances scream the way I made Fare scream last night, though. I don't hear my acquaintance's heart as I lie on their chest, the sound more important than anything in the world.

I think the High Prince and Niamh are distracted enough that I can say a brief goodbye.

Farron's eyes widen as I approach him. I can already hear his siblings arguing from inside the carriage.

"Hi," he says.

"Hi."

We've spent the whole last month together, our days and nights filled with laughter and adventures. I want to crash my lips against his one last time, taste the sweetness of his mouth. But that would reveal everything, share this treasure of a month with everyone.

Instead, I take his hands in mine, squeezing them tightly. "I'll see you at the Autumn Equinox Festival," I say, voice steady despite the ache in my chest. "And then at Winter Solstice."

"That feels so far away." Farron's smile is tinged with sadness. "You better be there."

"I will. I promise."

For a moment, we stand there, the world fading into the background. His gaze drops to my lips. I want to pull him close, to kiss him one last time, but the weight of our families' eyes feels too heavy. Instead, I release his hands and step back.

Farron lingers a little longer before he turns and opens the door to the carriage. The Autumn caravan begins to move. Their departure is torturous.

As the carriages roll away, the clatter of wheels and the sound of hooves filling the air, a sense of emptiness settles over me. I try to sort through my feelings. I've never been one to be content with a single lover, switching partners as often as I switch my clothes, sometimes entertaining more than one during the same night. But I didn't even think of another's flesh all month. My entire being craves him.

What do I do now until the Equinox? Remain celibate? I shudder at the thought.

But the notion of descending into one of the bars of Hadria, of losing myself in drink and sweaty skin…

Farron and I never said we would only be intimate with each other. What if he has a newfound fondness for it and explores back in Autumn?

My hands curl into fists, and I have a mind to race after his carriage and—

And what? Drop to one knee and beg him to make me his consort? To become a piece in this ever-rigid game of politics and princesses and princes? To lose the sea and the sand forever?

These weeks have been magical, but it's over now.

It's over.

I stand there long after the carriages have disappeared from view, the courtyard quiet once more. The rest of my family has left, and only my mother remains. Her long blond hair is curled and falls over her shoulders. She gives me a soft smile.

"Hey, Mom," I say.

"Hello, my baby," she says, wrapping her arms around me.

I lean down so my cheek rests on the crown of her head.

"I think that was a very productive embassy stay," my mother says. "We should invite Niamh and her family next year as well."

"We should."

"Her first-born son is quite the character."

I step back and raise a brow. "Careful, you're starting to sound like Dammy."

My mother smooths down my hair, the only one in the world capable of making it stay flat. "The High Prince notices political moves, issues with his trades and tariffs, but a mother"—her blue eyes glint—"a mother notices the lightness of her son's laugh, the ease of his smile, and the sparkle in his eyes. And who they often land upon."

I run a hand through my hair, messing it all up. "I have no idea what you're talking about."

Her knowing smile widens. "I have been blessed to find two great loves in my life. It's not something you should shy away from, no matter what difficulties there seem to be. My father himself fell for one of the Huntresses of Aura. The stories my grandmother told me of leaving her order to become a princess consort—"

"I still have no idea what you're talking about," I chide, but a fire burns beneath my ribs.

"Regardless, my darling boy, I know you." Her voice is soft as she says, "You've changed."

I close my eyes, the burning sensation next to my heart intensifying. "That's what I'm afraid of."

# 12

# FARRON

I wipe a bead of sweat off my brow, despite the mild weather. Maybe it's the constant clang of machinery, the giant mountain that looms over the city, or the clouds of smoke billowing from the forge, but there's something about Florendel, the capital city of the Spring Realm, that makes me nervous.

I know it's not the machines, the mountain, or the smoke that sends my pulse skittering, though. It's the person I need to speak to inside the forge.

The entrance to Draconhold Forge stands before me, a jagged opening that leads to the mountain tunnels within. I know the inside is akin to a beehive; hundreds of skilled workers craft the steel that's imported throughout the realms. We trade our lumber and bountiful harvests for their craftsmanship.

After leaving Hadria, my usual routine resumed in Coppershire. My family had been home for several fortnights before my mother wished to visit Florendel and asked me to accompany her. She claims it's a diplomatic mission, but I know she loves to visit Spring simply to catch up with her oldest friend, the High Princess Isidora.

Though I've visited Florendel countless times, Spring's High Princess always proves an imposing sight. Every time, she greets us from her throne, crafted of helms of the past High Rulers. I feel perpetually shrunken beneath the shadowed stare of her helm. However, once she and my mother retire to the study for discussion, they end up cackling away like two schoolgirls.

The Royal Family of Spring never removes their helms in front of anyone. On the way here, I asked Mother if she'd ever seen Isidora's face, and despite years of friendship, she said no, of course not. Then, she'd leaned in close and whispered that when the two of them are alone in the study, sometimes Isidora will lift her helm the smallest bit so she can take a sip of coffee. Mother said those slight glimpses of her jaw and mouth are sweeter than honey.

I'd much rather have been sitting in the study, drinking coffee, eating polvorones, and listening to Mother and Isidora gossip about the latest fashion trends in Summer or the marriageability of the young Winter Prince than have been sent off to the forge like an errand boy.

"Your lance is nearly complete," Isidora had gushed to my mother earlier. "My son is completing the final inspection of it today. He'll be in the forge. Farron, be a good lad and go fetch it. Your mother and I have much to discuss." Then they'd started giggling again, a sound quite foreign from my mother's lips.

"I don't know the way," I'd hedged.

Isidora had waved her hand. "I'll send my lady-in-waiting to show you."

Now, I stand before the gaping maw of the forge, throat tight.

"Well, what are you hesitating for, boy?" Isidora's lady-in-waiting asks. "There ain't no dragons inside! Get in there!"

I turn to the lady-in-waiting, a voluptuous red-faced woman with bouncy blond curls. Normally, I'd correct someone for not addressing me by my proper title, but there's something about this woman that makes me think I shouldn't cross her. "It's not dragons I'm worried about," I grumble.

"The prince will be working the Great Forge. Straight through. You won't be able to miss it," the lady-in-waiting says.

*That's* who I'm worried about. The prince. There's two of them.

The eldest isn't so bad. He acts like I don't exist, which is fine by me. But the youngest… I suppress a shiver. There's a quality to him that makes the hairs on the back of my neck stand up. *Please, oh please, oh please, let it be the older brother.*

Gulping, I turn to the lady-in-waiting. "Will you come with me, Ma—uh—Mary…"

"*Marigold!*" she snaps. "And you best remember it, boy. No, I don't go in there." She primps her ridiculously bouncy curls. "The soot affects my hair. You're a tough lad! Get in there!"

With that, she gives me an unceremonious shove on the back, and I stumble into the forge.

Heat and darkness swallow me as I step within Draconhold. I peer through the gloom. Bursts of bright orange light erupt on either side as workers stoke the massive forges, their hammers ringing out in a symphony of metal against metal. An acrid scent fills the cavernous space. Shadows dance across the walls, revealing glimpses of machinery and runes etched into the foundation. There's a scholar in the Scriptorium who can decipher Spring's runes and even speaks several of their unique languages. I'd like to learn one day.

Ahead, the Great Forge looms, a colossal structure that dominates the heart of Draconhold. Flames roar within its depths, casting an eerie glow that bathes the chamber in a fiery hue. A lone figure stands at the forge, only their silhouette visible, hammering on an object that gleams bright orange. Sparks fly with each strike.

My throat tightens. I can make out the silhouette now, a tall man who's wearing breeches covered in black smudges, a tight, sleeveless undershirt, and a leather apron.

And the helm, of course.

*What color is it? What color, what color?*

The man looks up from his work as I approach, and I breathe a sigh of relief. A silver helm. Not black. It's the eldest brother.

Prince Ezryn.

My whole body relaxes as I realize I won't have to have a painfully awkward experience with Kairyn, the younger brother. Now, I can just have a painfully awkward experience with Ezryn. Still embarrassing, but at least I won't feel like he wants to dismember me during the conversation.

Ezryn goes back to his work. This is the first time I've seen him without a full suit of armor. His arms bulge with each hammer swing, the muscles in his back rippling. His tawny skin is slick with sweat and smeared with oil. It's a wonder his mother hasn't paraded him around the marriage mart yet; I'm sure there'll be a line of suitors for the heir to the throne of Spring.

I walk up beside the forge and stand uncomfortably for what feels like eons. Ezryn doesn't look up again, merely continuing his relentless barrage against the red-hot sword before him. I wonder if he's seen me at all. He *can* see out of that helmet, can't he?

I wait another minute, then another, until the heat and clatter are too much for me to bear.

I fake a cough.

Ignored.

I fake a *louder* cough.

Ignored.

Finally, I step forward, leaning down so my face is close to the sword and wave. "Excuse me? Prince Ezryn?"

The hammer clangs one final time against the molten metal, then the Spring Prince places it to the side. His whole body stills, and I gulp. He feels like a predator, preparing to strike.

"Do you know how dangerous it is to be near an active forge without proper eye protection?" His voice reverberates from the helm.

I straighten and take a step back. "Uh, my name is Fare. Farron. Prince Farron. Of Autumn. I'm here to get—"

Ezryn turns his back on me, and I hold up my hands to prove I'm not actually invisible.

He reaches into a large chest and pulls out a gleaming lance. "A gift from Spring to the High Princess of Autumn. I forged this with my very hands. It is of the finest quality and will see Her Highness to victory in many battles."

"Great." I reach for it, but Ezryn yanks it back toward his body.

"Careful," he says coolly. "It's heavy."

What, because he's rippling with muscles and can work a forge and wears armor most of the time, he doesn't think that I can manage a lance? I narrow my gaze and hold my hands out for it.

Ezryn gives the slightest shrug of his shoulders then passes the weapon with one hand. I grab it with two. Immediately, the weight of it drags my whole body down, and its hilt slams on the stone ground, the sound ringing out in the din.

I can't see Ezryn's expression, but I get the distinct feeling he's scowling at me. Giving a sheepish grin, I hoist the lance up over my shoulder and turn to leave. "Thanks."

When I'm a few steps away, I hear his voice call out: "I can make you one, Prince Farron, if you wish."

I turn back. "I've got weapons in Autumn. Lots of them. Swords and bows and shields and, uh, flails, yeah, we've got those too—"

"The heir to the Autumn throne should wield a weapon of distinction," Ezryn says, words ringing out between the clangs of his hammer. "I crafted the blade that Keldarion of Winter wields, as well as various weapons for the three sons of Summer."

And just like that, with that single word, it all comes flooding back.

Summer.

The taste of salty ocean and sun-kissed skin. Sand, white as sugar, and water so reflective, I could make out the flecks of color in his eyes.

The Autumn Equinox came and went, and his whole family arrived, but Dayton wasn't there. I had begged and pleaded the staff to contact the head-of-house in Winter to see if he'd confirmed his attendance for the upcoming Winter Solstice event in Frostfang. Again, his whole family said they'd be there, except for him.

I've written letters that have gone unanswered. Stalked our tradesfolk for any update when they return from Hadria. My mother has begun grumbling it was a mistake to ever suggest this match at all.

Is Dayton avoiding me? Or maybe he's ill. I should go to him. Nurse him back to health. Or maybe he hates me, and I'd been a nuisance all along, one he was glad to be rid of.

Every day we've been apart, I've felt sick with longing for him. Like he kept a piece of me with him. I thought what we had meant more, especially after our night together on the isle. But it's like he's forgotten me.

I realize too long has passed since Ezryn asked me about the sword.. He's laid his hammer down and now sits on a stone bench, with a different sword and a whetstone in hand. I like the way I can't tell if he's looking at me through the helm, how I don't feel pressured to respond to him.

Dragging my feet, I shuffle up to the bench, lean the lance on the edge, then sit down beside Ezryn. He stiffens but goes back to sharpening the blade.

"Ezryn?"

He doesn't reply.

"Ezryn?"

"Yes?" he says gruffly.

"Your parents…they're fated mates, aren't they?"

"Yes."

"Have they ever talked about what it's, you know, *like*?"

"Not really."

I sigh. "Not even a little bit?"

Ezryn is silent for a few moments, the only sound the *ting* of the stone against the edge of the blade. Then he says lowly, "My mother believes in the old legends. That the souls of fae are born from matter of the heavens. That the hearts of fated mates fell from the same star. Though she doesn't speak of such things, I see the way she is with my father." Ezryn puts the sword and whetstone to the side, then turns to me, holding my gaze within the dark visor of his helm. "When they are with one another, it is to me as if they are part of the same constellation. Living starlight."

I hold my breath. Is that what I feel for Dayton? Like there're threads of starlight connecting us?

"Do you believe there's someone like that out there for you?" I ask.

Ezryn gives a low laugh. "I fear whatever star I've been cast from has not borne a heart suitable for such a thing."

"Mine neither," I mumble. Because even if I do feel all those things for Dayton, what does it matter? He can't even attend a party or respond to a letter.

Ezryn puts a hand on my shoulder. It's so strong and firm, I shrink beneath the weight. "You should return to Keep Hammergarden with the lance. Don't fret over the issue of fated mates or starlight. It is a phenomenon rarer than the most precious jewel; to wish for it is madness."

I stand and grab the lance. "You're right. Thanks, Ezryn."

Thinking about fated mates is madness, and pretending I might be connected to Dayton like that is even crazier. There's nothing tying us together but my own obsession.

I need to forget about the Prince of Summer before it breaks me apart.

# 13

## DAYTON

I'm hot. I'm too bloody hot.

And I fucking love the heat. But this fire is coming from the inside, and I don't know how to snuff it out.

Kicking, I toss my sheets off and gaze out the window. Pale pink light shines in. It's just past dawn then, a time when no sane fae should be awake, unless ending a night of celebration.

Groaning, I clutch at my chest. I cannot be ill, for I've seen a healer twice, with no cause for concern. Yet still, I feel like I'm on fire from daybreak until dusk.

Observing the rising sun, I am reminded of one fae who will be up and on duty. And for once, I could use his help.

I can't take this anymore. I'm in desperate need of relief, even if it means venturing into the place I hate most.

Quickly, I dress and leave my room.

"Damocles!" I call out, storming into his chambers. My brother looks up from his desk, eyebrows raised in surprise. "Take me to Castletree. Now."

He frowns. "What's going on?"

"I need to get to Winter." There's confusion in his eyes, but he doesn't argue.

Within moments, we're traversing through the door that connects Soltide Keep with Castletree, the ancient gateway between the realms. The grand staircase glimmers and a few of the staff stare down at us, curious about the situation.

Damocles shuts the door leading to Summer, then I twist the handle until the symbol above shows a snowflake. My breath comes in short, desperate gasps. "Open it. Please."

He does so, and we're greeted by a cool blast of air. The open door now reveals the halls of Keep Wolfhelm. Polished stone floors are adorned with thick rugs. I shiver but step through without hesitation, Damocles close behind.

My mind reels. I'm willingly in Winter, my least favorite of the realms—if you don't count the Below. I hate this place—the biting wind, the endless cold, the people even colder.

And speaking of cool, we round a corner to see the Prince of Ice himself.

Keldarion.

The man is a mountain of white. Taller than Damocles, his silvery hair falls past his waist. He wears a heavy fur cloak over tight leathers. His piercing blue eyes narrow as he sees us approach.

"What business do you have here?" Keldarion asks.

"This is my youngest brother's idea," Damocles says, and if I didn't know better, I'd swear there was amusement in his voice. Too bad my brother is incapable of such emotion.

Kel raises a brow at me but stays silent. Perhaps because he feels like I'm not even worthy speaking to or because he doesn't remember my name, I can't be sure.

Regardless, there's no point sidestepping what I need from him. "Take me to the coldest place you know, Keldarion. I need it. *Now*."

Keldarion glances at Damocles. "Is your brother mad?"

Damocles sighs, rubbing his temples. "Yes, but I like to humor Dayton's wild impulses from time to time. It keeps him from doing something even more ridiculous."

"At least I'm being ridiculous under your watch!" I snarl, the heat inside me flaring. "Now, Prince Keldarion, please, take me somewhere colder, because even your dick-shriveling keep isn't icy enough for me!"

Keldarion smirks. "Very well. Follow me."

WE TREK through the freezing halls and then out beyond the giant wall that surrounds Keep Wolfhelm. Damocles accepted the Winter Prince's offer of a cloak, but I refused. Gooseflesh covers my arms, and my teeth chatter.

But I'm *still* burning.

Outside of Frostfang, there's nothing but ice and snow as far as I can see. The only thing of interest is towering Mount Rhuvenmark, a long-dormant volcano. Keldarion leads us to a forest on the western side of the city. Eventually, we reach a vast lake, the surface so clear it looks like glass, reflecting the pine trees and tall, twisting mountains. Winter folk huddle over small circular holes, their rods dangling in the water.

"I don't know if this is the coldest," Keldarion says, judgment and confusion in his tone. "But at least it's within walking distance."

The air here is frigid, biting into my flesh with every breath.

"It's perfect," I say, slapping his back, which earns me an annoyed grunt.

Without a second thought, I strip off my shirt and stand before one of the abandoned holes. The water is so dark, it appears almost black. It's so unlike the clear turquoise ocean of Summer where you can see for miles beneath the waves, the coral sparkling pink, orange, and yellow.

I clench my hand over my burning heart and then lower myself into the water. The cold is shocking, a sharp, painful contrast to the fire that's been consuming me. I submerge myself, ducking under the surface.

Distantly, I hear the murmuring voices of my brother and Kel above. But I can't rise yet, not when it's still simmering within me.

An image flashes in my vision, auburn hair spread over my silken sheets, our bodies intertwined, his teeth biting into my shoulder as we move together.

I sink deeper.

Forge my own path.

That is *not* my future.

Another flash, this image right in front of me, so close I think there's someone there. A young woman falling, hands reaching for the surface, brown hair a tangle around her face. She's beautiful. She's drowning. I reach toward her, but she disappears in a hazy mist.

My heart feels on fire now.

Deeper. I push myself to the chilliest depths of this lake.

I stay there, letting the cold seep into every part of me, numbing the burning sensation that has tormented me for months. Finally, I feel the fire beside my heart begin to fade, replaced by a calming, divine frost.

As I emerge from the water, shivering but relieved, I look up at Keldarion and Damocles. "Thanks," I say through chattering teeth.

Keldarion shakes his head, a bemused expression on his face. "You, Dayton, are a mystery."

Damocles wraps a fur cloak around my shoulders, his eyes filled with a mix of concern and exasperation. "Let's get you back to the Summer Realm before you freeze to death."

"Thank you, Dammy," I say.

He stares at me, his blue eyes a mirror of my own. "You know I would do anything for you, little brother, even if I do not understand it."

"I know," I say. "And I'd do anything for you."

# 14

## FARRON

The carriage bumps along the cobblestone, the movement much rockier than the dirt road we were previously traveling on.

*We're almost there.*

I fold my hands in my lap. There's a wrinkle in my long gold tunic, and I smooth it out. We must look presentable today. It is a meeting of royals, after all.

On the seat across from me, my mother watches out the window. My little sister, Eleanor, sits beside her, reading a book.

My leg shakes up and down. I need to distract myself. We won't arrive for a while yet. Carefully, I grab my leather satchel. I brought a good book on the History of Human Relations. Lifting the buckle, a pop sounds, and a burst of smoke explodes in the carriage.

My mother gives a shriek of alarm, and my sister rolls her eyes without glancing up. A layer of dirt, twigs, and moss covers me.

My satchel had been booby-trapped.

Nerves give way to anger as I throw down the satchel, then open the carriage door. "Dom! Billy!" I frantically brush the mess off my finery and check for stains.

Childish laughter fills the air as Dominic and Billagin trot up on their ponies. The twins are nothing but mischief down to their hearts.

Dom offers me a sparkling grin. "We noticed how long you took getting ready this morning, big brother."

"Yes, we waited *hours* to get on the road." Billy chuckles.

I heave in a steadying breath. "It's difficult to look presentable while traveling."

It took seven days to pass from the Autumn to the Summer Realm. The landscape changes so drastically; one day we were surrounded by falling crisp red leaves, and the next, the air was thick and muggy, the trees blooming and green.

But today is our last day of travel. For quick visits between the realms, we always use Castletree as a gateway. We're able to get there quickly through the enchanted door in our keep, and then Castletree's magic allows us to access any of the four realms. However, for longer journeys, Mother and Father like to take the carriages so we can visit villages along the way. Father has friends everywhere, it seems, and Mother constantly reminds me of how important it is to understand your own people. She's right, of course, but all that socialization is exhausting. Finally, we're due to arrive in Hadria, the capital of the Summer Realm. Today, we will meet with the Royal Family.

"Boys." A clear voice fills the air as our mother pops her head out of the carriage. "Stop tormenting your brother. He's already nervous enough."

"Yes, Mumsie!" They plaster on matching grins before trotting off on their ponies.

"I'm not nervous." I fall back to my seat, crossing my arms over my chest.

My mother narrows her eyes at me and shuts the door. She's dressed in her finery, a cap-sleeved brown dress and a gold ribbon woven through her long chestnut and silver-streaked hair. "The Solstice Games are a grand celebration. They only occur every four years. All the royals will be there. Now come here, my clove."

I huff a breath at her pet name, but then begrudgingly slide between her and Eleanor. "You know what to expect. You've been to dozens of these. This is still new to me," I say.

"It was at a Winter Solstice that I met your father." My mother blows a gentle breeze, carrying dirt from my shoulder out a crack in the window. She weaves her long fingers through my hair, picking out the branches and twigs.

As if on cue, my father's thundering laugh echoes in the air. I catch his enormous frame outside, riding his massive brown horse. Probably chasing after the twins. His red beard and long hair blow in the wind.

"He was the captain of the guard accompanying us to Frostfang," my mother continues, "so my parents were unsure of the match at first. But when they saw how happy I was, they understood."

"I know the story." I sigh as my mother drops the last of the twigs onto her lap.

"Almost done." She smiles, then I feel the stir of her magic. The Blessing of Autumn. My own magic warms within me as the light brush of cold wind twines through my hair. "Eleanor, do you have a comb in your bag?"

My sister gives a long sigh and drags a string to mark her place in her book. Her hair, a smidge darker than mine, is braided into a crown on top of her head. "You know, he'd still kiss you, even with shit in your hair."

"Eleanor!" I snarl.

She rolls her bright gold eyes and shoves her bristle brush into our mother's hands.

Eleanor is not like the twins at all. She's calculating. Well, as calculating as a child of her age can be. If she could live in her books, she would. I suppose we have that in common. Though her preferred topics have always been a tad…questionable.

I peek a look at the title of her current read: *The Decaying Process of Small Mammals.*

My mother gives a sigh, bringing me back to the present moment. She brushes a section of my hair behind a pointed ear. "One day you'll understand, Nori."

Eleanor makes a disgusted sound in the back of her throat. "I'd rather be eaten by the Wyvern Tree and digested in its bark for the next thousand years."

And right now, I'm inclined to agree. Because the carriage rumbles to a stop and voices rise outside. We're here. We're at Soltide Keep.

*Fuck, fuck, fuck.*

It's been a year. What if he's forgotten me? He wasn't at the Autumn Equinox Festival or the Winter Solstice or the Spring Equinox, even though he promised he would be.

But he *will* be here.

I need to know if he's been consumed with memories of last summer like I have.

What happened between the kisses on the shore, where I'd given Dayton everything, and he swore he'd keep it safe? Was it all a play, just a game to him?

I can't believe that. Dayton may be a performer in the arena, but he couldn't have pretended the emotion in his eyes. So, what happened?

The door opens and the footman gestures for us to exit.

I heave in a breath and run a hand through my hair, distantly hearing my mother *tsk* about ruining all her hard work. But it's like my ears are stuffed with leaves, and all I can comprehend is the pounding of my heart.

The heat of Summer hits me like a wave as I stumble onto the sandstone street. Mother must have been keeping the carriage cool with her magic the whole time.

Here in the Summer Realm, I feel stifled. The blue sky is bright with white clouds, and ocean waves crash on the horizon. Officials line the streets. Before us lies glistening Soltide Keep.

Princess Sabine, long blond hair swinging loose, stands between her pair of chosen partners, Cenarius and Ovidius. High Prince Damocles is positioned next to his parents, skin bronzed and gleaming. Though he technically lives in Castletree, word has it he spends a great deal of time residing in Hadria, especially during times of celebration. Decimus stands at his side, back straight and chin held high.

I scan the line again. My mother pushes me into a bow as she greets the Summer royals, but I can't concentrate on anything. My heart aches.

He's not here.

Day isn't here.

# 15

## DAYTON

Warm air hits my face as my horse, Felix, gallops along the mountain hills. His easy canter knocks small pebbles down the cliffside and into the turbulent ocean below. It's still hot, despite it being nighttime.

"Ahh." I inhale a deep breath and stretch my aching arms. Justus gave me the training of a lifetime tonight.

*Reckless, emotional idiot.* All things he'd shouted at me earlier. But all I'd done was smile and laugh back. "I think what you're trying to describe, Master, is courage."

That had earned me a lap up the mountain carrying two goats on my shoulders and an hour of splitting firewood.

I can't blame him; I know he put pressure on me today because of the Solstice Games tomorrow. He'd never admit it, but he's worried.

He doesn't have to be.

His training is enough.

At least, I hope it is.

Buttery orange light spills out from Soltide Keep as I draw closer. Above, the stars sparkle like white shells in the sky. Guards wave and holler in greeting as I ride Felix into the stable, sliding off him as he bends to drink some well-deserved water.

"Daytonales." The deep voice shocks me to my core as my brother says my full name. I turn to look at him.

"Waiting for me, Decimus?"

My brother steps out of the darkness, moonlight illuminating his face. Compared to Damocles, Decimus is usually more lighthearted, easier to make laugh. But today, he looks like he's channeling our eldest brother. His mouth is a stern line, his dark brown eyes narrowed.

"Training with Justus again?" Decimus asks.

He's acting like the Imperator he is. Even off-duty, it seeps into his tone, his mannerisms. Everything he does is to protect the Summer Realm.

"Of course." I run my hand through my hair, full of dirt. Damn, I need to go to the baths. "The games begin tomorrow."

"Why do you think I'm concerned? These are not like other games, little brother."

"I know what type of games they are." I slap a hand on his shoulder and strut out of the stable. "I have borne witness to your and Damocles's competitions."

"Bearing witness is not the same as being in the arena under these stakes." My brother follows me.

"No," I say. An excited thrill runs through my body. "The roar of the crowd is never as loud as during the Solstice Games. I long for it."

Decimus sighs. "That's what I'm afraid of. How do you expect to win when you cannot even beat Damocles or me in a spar?"

"Fear not, Dec. I shall give the citizens of Summer a show they have not seen in an age."

"That's *also* what I'm afraid of." He gives me a serious look. "You missed another important arrival."

"Hmm?" I reach up to snag a low-hanging peach from a tree. "I'm sure none of those royal snobs noticed I was missing."

"It was the Royal Family of Autumn."

I still, the peach hovering before my lips. Alright, so maybe *one* person would notice.

"Ahh," I say and bite into the peach. "Where did you room them?"

"They're staying in the east villa."

I stare him down, swallowing the last of my peach, feeling the sticky sweetness drip down my chin.

"He's in the upper room. Coral suite."

Ice shivers through my veins, and for a moment, I think I'm back in Kel's damn lake. "Why would I care?"

Decimus's stern look cracks, and a smile flicks up his face. "I know you better than you think, Day."

"Does Damocles know?" We'd been so careful last year. At least, I thought we had. Though, Decimus has legions of loyal soldiers at his command. He knows everything about everyone.

"No, the High Prince has more pressing duties to worry about."

"Perfect." I force a grin, toss the peach pit into the garden, and walk away.

Decimus grabs my arm. "The Autumn Prince is not someone to engage in flighty dalliances with. Farron is next in line to be the High Prince of Autumn. Damocles and Niamh would be pleased if you were to officially court him. The match would be a favorable one."

I shake out of my brother's grip and scrunch up my face. "An official courting?" I manage a laugh. "It's just a bit of fun while he's here."

"A bit of fun?" Decimus's gaze pierces through me. "Is that why you've failed to attend every royal event he's been at since last Solstice?"

"I've been busy training for these games," I shoot back before I have time to consider his words.

Decimus shakes his head. "Try to get some rest, brother."

I wave my hand in the air as I make for the east villa.

Something strange vibrates in my blood. Why haven't I attended any of the royal events this year? It wasn't to avoid Farron. There was always something pressing at home. More training to be done. Goats to brush. Parties to attend. Important things.

Maybe it was because I was so afraid of burning up inside again.

But if I don't care, why does it feel like I can't move fast enough?

I stop in front of the sandstone towers of the villa. I don't want to waste time talking to the guards or introducing myself to any Autumn nobility who could still be awake, so I walk beneath the balcony of the coral suite. A curling line of ivy runs down the side of the building, which I scale. Much easier than his last room, which stuck out over the sea.

I hop onto the balcony and pass through the sheer curtains.

Vibrant tapestries adorn the white columns and pale stone walls. Against the far wall is a large four-poster bed with a canopy of gauzy fabric that sways in time with the balmy night breeze.

The candles are dim, and it takes a moment for my eyes to make sense of the room. Then I see him.

Something unclenches in my ribcage.

Farron is sprawled on the bed, with one leg hanging out of the covers and his auburn hair forming a messy halo around his face. His eyes are closed, and his chest rises and falls in an even cadence. There's an open book in his hand.

A small smile tugs at the corner of my mouth. The idiot probably fell asleep reading.

I didn't mean to avoid him for an entire year. It was just that I didn't know what to do when I saw him again.

Fuck, I still don't know what to do. How am I supposed to act after everything that happened last year? After he nuzzled into my neck when we finished fucking? After staying up all night talking and watching the stars? After knowing he smells like fresh apples and cinnamon with kisses just as sweet?

Nothing about last Solstice had been normal. There were so many firsts I showed him.

And it's been an entire year since I've seen him.

A knot forms in my stomach. Look at me. Finding him the exact moment he's within reach.

He's lying before me like some sort of dream. Slowly, I pad close to the bed, then bend a knee and lean over. I don't know if I want to wake him or watch him.

All I know is I must get closer.

Carefully, I brush a line of hair away from his brow.

He jerks, golden eyes shooting open, and hits me in the face with his book.

# 16

## FARRON

A deep grumble sounds in the air, and a man falls off the bed, clutching his nose. Blood runs out from between his fingers.

"Dayton?"

"*Fuck,*" he groans, lowering his bloody hands. "Did you hit me with a fucking brick?"

"It was the entire poetic work of Tarragon Wrinklelake," I say, looking down at the large tome. "So, yes, in a sense."

"Do you often assault people in your bedroom?"

"Do you often creep into your guests' quarters in the middle of the night?"

He gives a deep laugh. "Only the cute ones."

My traitorous cheeks burn, and I fall back to the bed, eyeing him. He's filthy, dirt covering his loose pants and bare chest. Of course Dayton wouldn't bother with a shirt. His long blond hair falls over his shoulders in messy waves. How is it possible he's even more gorgeous than I remember?

A bone-deep ache runs through me at the sight of him, and I can't seem to catch my breath. He is real. A part of me feared I'd made him up, or I'd gone mad last summer, and he never existed at all. But he's here. With me.

I don't know if I should scream or cry or smile or laugh.

"What are you doing here?" I finally ask, impressed I can even form words.

He walks off, an almost awkward gait to his movements. "Didn't realize you arrived today."

"The rest of your family was there."

"Right." He lets out a long breath. "I was training for the games tomorrow. Got someone in the audience I want to impress."

I have to look away. He's…flirting with me? I haven't heard from him in a year. Not a single word of reply to any of the letters that I sent.

But what did I expect? An apology for whisking me away and making me feel like I was special, only to have my heart shattered every single day that passed when I heard nothing from him?

Yet, my stupid heart still swoons at his smile.

"You were not so diligent about training last year," I say.

"Well, that's your fault. There was too much to show you. The ocean, the islands." His voice is a purr.

I hold my breath, remembering the turquoise water, feeling the soft sand beneath my back as he kissed my neck, his naked body above me glistening with sweat and seawater…

I shift, making sure my legs are covered with the thin blankets, hoping it's dark enough to hide my hardening length.

"Do you remember one particular island? Captain Katharine's Isle?" The bed dips as Dayton lowers before me, his breath warm, the scent of salt and—

"You smell like goat," I snap at him.

He pulls back, lifting an arm. "I should take you with me to see Justus one of these days. You'd like the goats. And I think he'd like you."

Was that what he wanted, really? For me to return and have things be like they were last summer? Has he even thought of me this past year?

Has he been with anyone else?

I shake my head, ignoring his comment. Of course he has been with others. I know him.

I'd tried to move on, too. After the Winter Solstice, when it was clear he had no intention of seeing me again, I resolved to forget about him. But no one piqued my interest.

A calloused hand tucks a strand of hair behind my ear as he leans closer. Perhaps the smell of goat isn't so bad. "There are more places I want to show you, Fare. Other things I want to do."

My breath hitches in my throat. It would be so easy to fall back into this. But he hasn't even offered an explanation. Hasn't even said sorry.

I don't want to feel how I felt when he didn't show up at the Autumn Equinox. The Winter Solstice. Every event since.

It's clear the Summer Prince and I want different things.

Not that I'm entirely sure what I want from him.

I scoot back on the bed. "I won't have as much time on this trip. My mother wants me to inherit the Blessing soon. I'll be shadowing her and spending time with the High Prince."

Dayton blinks at me. It's clear from his expression that he is seldom rejected.

When he says nothing, I continue, "You fight in the arena tomorrow, correct? That's what your family said at the welcome dinner. I'm sure you need to rest."

Dayton straightens, and I hate that my body already aches to be close to him. That I want to call out for him to stay.

"Right," he says, voice hoarse. He walks to the balcony, not even going to leave the normal way.

He looks back at me over his shoulder, blue eyes glinting in the moonlight. "I want to hear you cheer from the box tomorrow, Fare." Then, in a fluid motion, he throws himself over the edge of the balcony and swings down the vines.

I clench the sheets of my bed and whisper, "Of course I'll cheer, you idiot."

I'D THOUGHT the villa was hot, the wind blowing a breeze meant for high noon in the middle of the night. I'd thought the streets of the capital were warm, waves of heat making my vision swim. But the Sun Colosseum burns as if we are on the surface of the sun itself.

I'm on a high balcony with the other royals. On a tier above us sit the High Princes and Princesses, the small children lounging in chairs around them. I, however, have been seated with the other nobles on the lower tier. It is a terrace hanging right above the arena with little covering.

Around us, the Sun Colosseum is packed with what must be every single citizen of Hadria. Below, on the white sand, fighting with magic and weapons, are two gladiators. Whoever wins this fight will compete in the finale of the games and have a chance at the title of Champion.

I watch the battle with a mix of fascination and squeamishness as the two fighters clash their weapons in a dazzling display of strength and skill. Despite the intensity of the battle, there is some grace and beauty to the warriors' movements as they leap and parry. A deadly dance.

I fall back in my chair, fanning my sweaty forehead with a paper fan.

If there's any consolation to the blazing heat, it's that I'm not the most miserable one here. The heir to Winter takes low, shallow breaths, sweat dripping down the planes of his chiseled jaw. He wears his white hair loose; it's so long it trails down to his waist.

I can barely breathe when I look at him—a mixture of jealousy, envy, and awe swirl within me.

Keldarion is everything an heir should be: brave, handsome, righteous. He's slightly older than me and is already commanding his realm's army. When the spiders of Frosthold Crag kidnapped a prestigious lady, he led a mission with only one other to rescue her. Not to mention he's making political gains with his courtship of a noble in the Spring Realm.

Lady Tilla walks down the steps, her long black hair tied in intricate braids atop her head.

"Here, darling." She hands Keldarion a glass of cold water. He gives a grunt of approval before waving his hand above it. The water changes to bits of snow, which he blows into his face.

Only a trifle of his power. He might not have inherited Winter's Blessing yet, but I've heard stories of the power at his command.

He's the heir I should be. The kind the Autumn Realm deserves.

Tilla sits down beside him. Since she's not part of the Spring Realm's royal house, she's not bound to the faceless armor the way the royal line is. She's beautiful, her tawny skin made up with rouge, dark eyes lined with kohl. She honors Spring's traditions in her clothing. A metal circlet sits atop her head, and dark steel swoops to sharp points on her shoulders. A chain mail belt ties together her pink dress.

If the rumors are true, she knows the ways of the Spring Realm and is a warrior in her own right.

My gaze slides to the two Spring Princes sitting next to me. I can't help the fear that trembles up my body as I take in their massive, armored forms. One silver. One black. They both sit still as mountains.

Ezryn and I haven't exchanged as much as ten words since I saw him last year. I always thought that was his entire personality, but I caught him laughing with Keldarion earlier.

As Winter is lucky to have Keldarion, so is Spring to have Ezryn. Word traveled that when a strange blight destroyed Spring's crops, the High Princess trusted him alone to assist her in bringing life back to the dead earth.

I can't dwell on it for long because the arena shakes as the crowd erupts in a massive cheer. Below, the battle has finished. A huge gladiator has his hammer pressed to the chest of another fae on the ground who holds his finger up in surrender.

"Spiculus." Decimus, the middle brother of the Summer Royal Family, leans over to tell me. "A worthy opponent for the final match."

"That's who Dayton will face to become Champion?" I ask.

"If he wins his next fight." Decimus grins at me as if we share an inside joke. We both know Day will win. The way he's been fighting today...

I've never been much for violence, but seeing him compete this morning—and win again and again and again—has filled me with a strange elation.

As if on cue, the crowd erupts in a frenzied commotion, and the name Daytonales echoes throughout the arena as the citizens of Summer cheer for their prince.

I push myself up from my seat and clutch the edge of the balcony as Dayton steps upon the sand. A wild smile dances on his face as he raises his dual swords in the air. Across the arena, his opponent walks forward, banging his sword against his shield.

I've always thought of Dayton as huge, with his broad shoulders and tall stature, but his opponent looks like a giant of legend. His shadow stretches wide across the sand.

But Dayton doesn't care. He turns in a circle, grinning wildly and pumping his sword toward the crowd. The people ignite like leaves in a forest fire, screaming and hooting. I even spot one woman yank down her dress and flash her breasts.

The hulking behemoth across from Dayton is no showman. His eyes are stern and focused.

*Pay attention, you idiot,* I think.

Dayton flicks one look up to the royal box—probably searching for his brother—then surges. He's all coiled energy and dazzling grin. His swords sparkle left-right-up-left, deftly avoiding the other gladiator's huge shield. The crowd roils like a stormy sea, their chorus of cheers resonating throughout the arena.

The giant fae roars, and now Dayton is on defense. He dodges expertly, the other gladiator heaving his sword down in slow, powerful arcs.

The taste of blood wafts over my tongue, and I realize I've chewed my nail down to the quick. *Why am I so nervous?*

The larger gladiator can't get a hit. Dayton keeps rolling away, then smacking from behind, only to turn and grin up at the crowd.

"He's playing with him," Keldarion grunts out. "Classless."

"Oh, I don't know," Tilla says. "The skill with which he's wielding those blades is unmatched. If I could get a better look at them…"

Dayton leaps away from every swing, laughing and smiling at the spectators—as if their cheers and applause are all the energy he needs to keep going.

"What kind of madman laughs while he fights?" a tinny, cold voice says, drawing my attention. A cool shadow falls over me as the youngest Prince of Spring, Kairyn, stands at my side.

My sweat turns icy as I look up at his armored face. His mask has always reminded me of an owl with two extended protrusions over the dark visor that look like feathered eyebrows. But the shape is almost completely obscured by his black hood.

*How does he not boil in that thing?* I wonder as my eyes trail over the intricate black armor adorned with silver filigree, the cape that puddles on the floor like spilled oil. It's as if he absorbs the surrounding light, the visor where his eyes should be like a pool of dark water, deep and inscrutable.

"I've always thought his laughter hides his fear." The heir to the Spring Realm steps up beside his brother, and I feel more at ease. His silver armor, with the beautiful floral designs, glitters in the high sun. "But perhaps he truly is mad."

"No," I breathe and turn back to the fight, watching Dayton dance around the other gladiator, so light on his feet. "It's who Day is. He's not thinking or pretending. He lives only in the present moment. There is nothing for him except the sword and the crowd. When Dayton is doing something, he's there completely. He's living."

Maybe that's why those moments together last summer were so special to me. Because I knew there was no one else that mattered to him but me. To exist like that—wholly taken away from your problems, if only for a little while—was euphoric.

The hulking gladiator is bent double, panting, and Dayton takes the opportunity to stroll toward the crowd, basking in their cheers like they're a healing balm. Even from here, I can see the sweat dripping down his chest.

Dayton throws his head back and laughs as the spectators chant his name. But the other gladiator has regained his composure. He hulks behind him, massive weapon raised. Dayton doesn't notice. He's looking up at the crowd.

"Dayton!" I cry.

The huge gladiator brings down his sword, and Dayton turns at the last second. He dodges out of the way, but the blade nicks his shoulder, and a drop of red blood ekes onto the sand.

Something switches in Dayton's form, and although we're too far above to see, I can feel the darkness falling over his gaze. He ignites, rushing forward, and in two vicious blows, his opponent crumbles to his knees.

The massive gladiator holds a single finger up in surrender, and the Colosseum shakes with the roar of the crowd. Dayton tilts his head up at the box, and I swear he's looking straight at me as he winks.

Dayton is the victor. He is going to proceed to the last battle for the chance to take the title of Champion.

"Hmm," Keldarion grumbles and leans over the banister with the rest of us. I take a moment to look from him to Ezryn, then down at myself. One day, the three of us will rule as High Princes alongside Dayton's oldest brother, Damocles.

I am unworthy.

"An interesting theory you gave, little prince," Keldarion says. He looks down at the arena, as if the whole thing is distasteful to him. "We will see if he's still laughing when there is true blood to be spilled."

Kairyn gives a low laugh, echoing strangely beneath his mask. "It is the way they should always fight. None of this surrender. There is no way to test a fae's merit without life on the line."

A pit settles in my stomach, and I turn to them. "What do you mean?"

"I thought you knew." Decimus places a hand on my shoulder. "The final fight of the Solstice Games is to the death."

# 17

## DAYTON

The glorious smell of sweat and blood fills my nose. Hands clap me on the back and congrats ring in the air. I walk among my fellow gladiators as we crowd in the corridors beneath the Sun Colosseum.

Soon, I'll compete in the final match and claim victory in the Solstice Games, as my brothers have in years past. My gaze darts around the din to see Spiculus sitting in a corner. A serene look floats across his face. He's meditating.

Scars mark his body. I'm not sure he's ever been defeated in a game.

But neither have I.

A low murmur of voices carries through the corridor and prickles the back of my neck. Whistling, jeers.

"Is this a new prize?"

"What tender meat."

Every nerve in my body is filled with tension, and I push through the crowd to see him.

Farron stands dwarfed in a throng of gladiators, all taunting and laughing at his awkwardness.

"What are you doing here?" I'm surprised by the venom in my voice, and it carries enough power that everyone backs away from us.

He blinks his gold eyes up at me. "I was trying to find you."

Suddenly, I'm not sure I can wait to get into the arena to fight. All the surrounding people seem like the enemy. As soon as I grip his arm and pull him toward me, I feel better. But it's not enough.

I drag Farron down a set of stairs, then through the maze of corridors and halls until I stop before an inconspicuous wall.

"Where are we—" Farron starts.

"Shut up." I place my palm on the stone. It flashes a bright emblem of the sun before it pushes inward, and the bricks move aside to reveal a door.

Farron blinks wildly before I pull him through. "These are private dungeons, only accessible to the royal line," I explain as the door closes behind us. "We used to house the vilest of criminals here before execution in the arena."

The sandy cell is dimly lit with a narrow crack of light slicing through the darkness. Through the crack, I catch sight of the blood-soaked sand and the crowded stands. Cheers and shouts echo through the rock. The grime of past prisoners stains the jagged walls. A thick set of chains, rusted and worn, are bolted to the sandstone. They hang from the ceiling, looped through heavy iron rings, as if waiting for their next occupant. The crack of light serves as a cruel reminder of the world beyond, taunting the prisoner with a glimpse of freedom.

"Why did you bring me here?" Farron asks at the same time as I growl, "Why did you come here?"

We stare at each other until I sigh. "I didn't like the way they were looking at you."

His eyes are glassy. I step toward him.

"Why didn't you tell me the games are to the death?" Anger tremors in his voice.

I recoil, raising my hands in a peaceful gesture. "I thought you knew."

He shakes his head, wild hair falling into his eyes. "I thought it was like all the other games you told me about—with surrendering!"

"It's okay," I tell him. "I've never lost."

"But if you lose this time, it's your *life*."

I grip his face between my hands. "You don't understand, Fare. Death during the Solstice Games is not something to fear. If my blood soaks the sands, then my memories will live on forever in the Orb of Ancestors."

He slips out of my grasp. "You'd rather be stuck in an orb than with me?"

"Well, it wouldn't be *me,* just a memory of me. But that's not the point. This is a sacred celebration. Both my brothers have competed and won in games prior. It is my turn now."

Farron pivots, running his hand over the chains that hang from the wall. A large brass key sits against the stone, and he pushes it around with his toe. "I don't like it."

I pull him against my chest. "It's okay. You can say you're worried about me."

Tension releases from his body, and every part of me wonders how I went so long without this.

From the small crack that lets in the arena's light, I hear the crowd cheer.

"Come on," I murmur against his neck before I pull away. "I have to go."

I walk to the stone door and press my palm against a brick. The sun emblem lights beneath my hand, and the entrance opens.

And then I realize Farron's not beside me. There's a clicking sound, and I turn back to see both of Farron's hands are clasped in the cuffs.

"What are you doing?" I rush back to him, grabbing the key from the floor. "Look, stop messing around."

"I'm staying here until the match is over."

I look him up and down. There's a determined power to the set of his face. It's the same look as when he jumped off the cliff.

"Are you crazy?" I roar. "If I lose, no one will find you down here."

"Then don't fucking lose."

# 18

## FARRON

The chains are heavy on my arms, and I strain at the bindings. Cheers grow in intensity, and I know Dayton must be stepping onto the sand.

*Stupid, stupid, stupid.* What was I thinking, chaining myself to the wall? The only way out of this cell is closed now. If he falls in combat, there won't be just one princely death.

I hear the clang of metal and more shouts as the battle outside begins. Closing my eyes, I listen to the sounds of the fight. I picture Dayton, the way he moved across the sands in that Sun Colosseum, his hair flying in golden waves. The grin spreading over his face as he swipes his sword.

Every cry from the crowd has my whole body shaking. I try to analyze what each cheer means. Surely, they must be rooting for their prince.

The blood rushes through my head and limbs, so hot I can barely think.

My wrists burn, my arms ache. The chains are welded to the wall, and no amount of struggle will tear them loose.

It happens so quickly, I almost don't register it.

There's a roar from the crowd that's different from all the others, and then chanting, but I can't make out the name from the ringing in my ears.

No… No.

My stomach twists. A stream of blood trickles through the crack in the wall and drips upon the floor.

I heave in great, gasping breaths. He has to be okay. He has to be…

Suddenly, the stones shift, and there is a silhouette standing there. And for one wild moment, I think it's Aeneas, the first High Prince of Summer, for he looks so mighty. A prince of the arena.

But he steps forward, and the warm line of light illuminates Dayton's face. His chest is splattered with blood.

He's won.

And he didn't wait a moment to bask in his victory on the sands.

He came to me.

# 19

## DAYTON

Farron blinks at me, tears pooling in his eyes. I cross to him in two steps.

My chest still heaves with the exertion of the fight, the thrill of the battle coursing through my veins.

The final match was unlike anything I'd experienced in my entire life. I ended it quickly, efficiently, in a way that would have made Justus proud. With every strike of my sword, I thought of Farron. People love to call me an idiot, but what kind of person locks themselves in a cell?

Why had he done that?

I grab his face and press my lips to his cheek. "I won."

Outside, I can still hear the chanting of my name. I'll have to return to accept my victory soon. But the only thing that mattered was getting back to him.

"You won," he murmurs against my skin.

"Let's get you out of here," I say, looking at the corner of the cell where I left the key.

"I can't wait." Farron surges forward, crashing his lips against mine.

The kiss is intense and untamed, and it's precisely how I crave it. I feel like I've won so much more than the fight. Farron shivers against me, his body pressing into mine.

I pull away, my eyes tracking up to his, seeing his hands dangling above his head. "Hmm, I don't want to release you yet."

His eyes widen, and he gives a little moan of pleasure. Slowly, I kneel and open the golden buttons of his tunic, trailing my tongue down his soft skin before I stop above the waistband of his pants.

"Would you like me to touch you, Fare?"

"Yes." He bucks his hips closer to my face. I can feel his hardness through his slacks; my own cock aches in similar fashion.

"Fuck," I groan and strip his pants down to his boots. And damn if his cock isn't gorgeous, hard and long and dripping with precum. "Does the thrill of battle make you ache, Farron?"

His breathing grows ragged as I stroke him slowly. "I need you."

My eyes meet his, and I can see the sincerity in them. I lean forward, my lips grazing his length before I take him in my mouth, tasting his salty sweetness.

Farron moans, his hips thrusting as I move my lips up and down his hardness.

He makes a sound of pleasure as I run my tongue around the tip of his cock. His body trembles. He's close. The thought ignites a primal ferocity within me.

I pull away, looking up with a satisfied smirk. "Now I'm definitely not letting you out of these chains."

Then I take his entire length to the back of my throat.

He lets out a deep moan, and his hot seed explodes in my mouth. I swallow greedily, and when he's spent, I lick his cock clean. Fuck, he tastes amazing.

I stroke his still-twitching member. My hand continues its slow teasing.

"Please, Dayton," Farron begs. He must know I can't deny him a thing. "I need you inside me."

I stand and push the leather down my legs, my cock on full display. Spitting on my fingers, I press my shaft against his stomach and reach around to stroke his entrance.

"You ready for me, Fare?"

He nods, wild hair falling in his face.

I lift him, pressing him to the sandstone wall. He wraps his legs around my waist. My hard length pushes against his entrance. He gasps, his eyes fluttering closed as I slide inside. We both moan as I thrust deep, filling him.

I drive into him hard, our moans echoing off the chamber. His body quivers beneath me as he makes his way closer and closer to the edge.

I never come in my lovers. Had never done so before until my first time with him. Something about it feels too intimate. Too lasting. But every ounce of me wants to fill him with my seed again, wants to claim him. Mark him in a way no one else can.

"Fuck." My pace increases at the thought of my cock exploding in his ass.

"Day," Farron cries out, face scrunching.

I pull him close, my mouth dipping to his neck to suck on the sensitive skin. I need to possess him, make him mine, fill him, scar him.

If anyone ever lays a hand on him, I'll rid them of life and fuck him in their blood.

A broken moan escapes his lips as I release my teeth from his neck. A red mark lingers. *Good.*

The chains rattle in time with the slap of our bodies, my balls hitting his ass hard as I push as deep as I can go. *Not hard enough.* Strength courses through my arms as I grab his hips, pulling him down more. Then I still.

Arching my back, I let out an intense moan as I feel his tight muscles grip my cock. His whimpering voice is so sweet. "Oh gods, Day. Fuck, fuck, fuck."

But I don't move, not yet. I stare at him, firmly gripping the nape of his neck. His whole body shudders around my length, his own cock hard again and aching, dripping against his stomach.

"Day... Day," he breathes.

"Shush." My fingers tremble on his hips, tight enough to bruise. "I want to feel this, Fare. I need to feel this. Just for a little longer."

He nods, hands grasping the chains. "This feels so good. You feel so good."

I squat down, still holding Fare close to me, and grab the key off the floor. Trembling, I unlock the chains from the wall, and his wrists fall away to loop around my shoulders. We both let out a moan as the movement pushes me deeper inside him. He's so easy to hold in my arms. His mouth opens against me as I kiss him. I rotate my hips, not ready to pull out even an inch. I circle my cock, touching every part of his inner walls.

Farron kisses me deeply, then sucks on my bottom lip before biting down.

"Naughty boy," I murmur. "I'm going to fucking fill you to the brim, baby, until you're stuffed full of my cum."

His reaction to my words spasms through his whole body. His muscles clench so hard around my cock, I almost explode.

"Would you like that?" I groan. "You'll have to walk out of here with my cum running down your legs."

He blinks, eyes glassy, face flushed. He's too fucking cute, too fucking beautiful. I never want to let him go. I move my lips to his ear. "Walk past all those gladiators. They won't see it. But they'll smell it. They'll know who you belong to."

Farron whips his head to capture my lips with his, his soft hair falling across my brow. He moans something. I think it's yes. But I need to make sure.

I pull out, out, out, out, out of him, until it's just my tip nudging his entrance. It's delicious how his body moves and squirms with the movement.

"Tell me, who do you belong to?" I plunge all the way into him. His answer is a broken whimper. I pull out again, slamming in harder. "Tell me, baby."

Farron's face scrunches up and he lets loose a cry. His fingers are so tight in my hair I swear he almost pulls it out.

My pace increases rapidly, strong strokes deep inside him. "Tell. Me. Who. You. Belong. To," I growl at him with each pump.

"Day, I'm yours." He grips my face with sweat-slicked palms, then brings his lips before mine. "I'd crawl naked behind you if you asked."

*Fuck.* His cock is so hard. I free my hand from his waist to touch him. He's so ready for me, all it takes is that one hard stroke for ropes of his sticky hot release to coat my palm.

The shattering of his face sends me over the edge. I push deeper than I have all night, roaring as I burst inside him.

"Day," Farron groans, wiggling in my arms.

"You're not moving." I pull him closer. "Not until you take it all."

"Fucking fill me, Day. It feels so good. Gods!"

My cock keeps shuddering into him, waves of pleasure releasing. Something tightens in my chest at his expression. That half-lidded gaze he's giving me…

He needs to stop looking at me like that.

I kiss him, but it's not like I expected. His lips are so soft. And I'm falling. We're falling, to the sandy ground, and I'm still inside him. I never want to leave. He's clutching my face, and when he pulls away, he whispers, "I'm so glad you won."

Of course I did.

Because I know something now.

I won for him.

There is nothing I wouldn't do for him.

And damn to the gods if that isn't more frightening than fighting to the death in the arena.

# 20

## FARRON

The throne room of the Serenus Dusk Chambers is alive with celebration. The very air feels electric as the Summer and Autumn royal families, as well as chosen friends, drink, dance, and praise Dayton's victory. Laughter and music abound, and I'm swept up in the pure joy of it.

The Serenus Dusk Chambers are the private quarters attached to the back of the Sun Colosseum. They feel moodier, more intimate, than the huge sprawling coral rooms of Soltide Keep. Night has fallen, and flickering torches dimly light the space. It's crowded, but for once, I don't mind.

Not when I have Dayton by my side.

Bobbing blue lights drift overhead. They look like living flames, flitting about. "Dayton, are those—"

Dayton puts his head on my shoulder and follows my gaze. "The blue lights? They're spirits of our ancestors. They're drawn to great gatherings of life. Wonderful, aren't they?"

I narrow my eyes. I recognize them from a book I've read. In Autumn, we call them will-o'-wisps. Apparently, they've been seen in the Emberwood, not that I've been lucky enough to encounter one. The book says they are the wayward hearts of mated souls who never completed their bond, but I like Dayton's explanation better, so I don't say anything.

People come up to congratulate Dayton, and he beams with pride. My heart swells, seeing him so happy. His joy is contagious. Despite the constant attention, he never strays from my side. If he's called somewhere, he pulls me along.

The ringing of a glass sounds, and I look up to see one of Dayton's fathers, Ovidius, and his mother, Sabine, standing on the pedestal by the throne. Ovidius has his arm around Sabine's shoulders, and she smiles so wide, it's as warm as the sun itself. The crowd quiets and turns to face them.

"On this happy day, we have more joyous news to share," Ovidius calls out.

Sabine sprawls her hands across her stomach. "We are expecting another child. I feel her heart already. It is a girl."

There's a breath of silence, and then the crowd erupts into cheers. Dayton gives a near ear-splitting shriek, then looks around frantically. He spots his brothers, Damocles and Decimus, and sprints over to them. The three brothers scream and holler like wild animals, wrapping their arms around one another until they form a circle, jumping up and down. I can't help but burst out laughing at the sight.

Cenarius, Dayton's other father, runs up to the throne and kisses Sabine passionately. Then he goes to Ovidius, grasping his arm. "We're to share a daughter!"

Finally, the brothers make it up to their parents, and the family embraces one another. Their joy is so palpable, the whole crowd is moved. From across the room, I catch eyes with my mother, who smiles and picks Nori up into her arms for a squeeze.

Watching Dayton and his family together, the love that radiates between them… It reminds me how much goodness is in the world. How much joy there is to find. All of my problems seem so small compared to this happiness.

After a few minutes, Dayton breaks away from his family. The crowd parts for him as he strides over to me. I'm struck still by the confidence in his gait, the surety with which he walks to me.

"I'm so happy you're here, Fare," he says.

Then he places his hands on the sides of my face and kisses me.

Kisses me in front of everyone, for all to see.

I melt into his embrace. I matter to him. Matter more than undermining Damocles. Matter enough to show his family what we are to one another.

I kiss my boy back and he tastes like starlight.

# 21

## DAYTON

The steady, calm waves draw me from sleep. The sun's warmth caresses my face, and beside me, I hear soft breath and the tinkle of shells.

Slowly, I blink my eyes open and see Farron lying on his stomach, hands busy with seashells and twine.

"Looks like I fell asleep." I groan, stretching my arms high above my head.

Farron sets down what he's working on and leans over me until we're nose to nose. "Did I wear the mighty warrior out?"

He flashes a mischievous grin, and I can think of so many ways to knock it off his face. I settle with grabbing the nape of his neck and pushing his lips against mine, kissing him deeply. "What can I say?" I murmur against his mouth. "It takes a lot of work to satisfy an Autumn Prince."

Farron gives a deep sigh that has my whole body craving his. I grab his shoulders and roll us until he's below me on the sand.

Four weeks have passed since his family arrived in the Summer Realm, and the time has changed him. Red gleams in his auburn hair, and his skin has the faintest hint of color. He blinks up at me, and I can't help but notice the flash of sadness in his eyes.

I know what it's about. I roll off him and sit up. We'd spent the day on Captain Katharine's Isle, this time taking my small skiff instead of swimming. I haven't seen a kelpie this time, though, so maybe Farron really did lead it home.

It's sunset now. How long have I slept? The waves roll, cresting with sparkling light, and the sand beneath my fingers shines like pink diamonds.

I run my hand through it and see Farron must have traced patterns with a stick while I slept. "Roses, Fare?"

"Hmm?" He sits up and looks over at me.

I gesture to the myriad of swirling roses drawn in the sand. "Is this your way of hinting you want me to get you flowers?"

He flushes as pink as the setting sun. "They're my favorite flower. I've always thought they were the most beautiful."

"Roses grow inside of Castletree," I tell him. "I'll get you one next time we go."

"I've seen them," he says, then his voice wavers. "Will you be there for the Rainbow Eclipse Festival?"

*He's nervous because after his visit last summer, I didn't see him at all.* I grab his chin and make him look up at me. "I told you I'd get you a rose, didn't I?"

He shakes his head before launching at me and crashing our mouths together. The kiss is heady and desperate, and he murmurs, "I wish I didn't leave tomorrow."

"I wish you didn't either."

And damn if I don't mean it. If last summer with him had been incredible, this summer has been mind-blowing. And not just the sex —which was fucking euphoric. I've never felt as connected with someone as I am with him. We'd spent our days exploring the Summer Realm, mostly the small islands, markets, and vineyards. I'd even taken Fare up the hills while I trained with Justus. Turns out Justus isn't a crotchety old bastard to everyone. In fact, to Fare, he's as pleasant as an old grandfather. Or maybe Farron has the magic to melt anyone with his sweet smile and soft words.

It still didn't stop Justus from putting me through the wringer with his training, only I had two people judging me instead of one. And the goats, of course.

Even the boring noble shit we have to do doesn't seem so bad when Farron's around. Both my brothers adore him, even if Decimus likes to rough him up a little in typical older brother fashion. Mother is smitten. Farron spent an entire day with her in the library as they looked up possible names for my expected new sister. And my fathers kept giving me strange looks whenever they caught us together, like they know something I don't.

And maybe they do.

I thought I'd never hear the end of it from Damocles, that he'd be chasing me through the halls with a marriage contract. But instead, he's been unexpectedly nice to me. He's barely mentioned anything about it at all.

"Come with me," Farron breathes against my neck.

"What?" I pull back.

His lip trembles, but something glimmers in his eyes. "Come home to the Autumn Realm with me."

When I don't respond, he blinks rapidly, then looks down. "Y-you could say you're visiting on…on a diplomacy trip."

My words are achingly slow. "Are you suggesting I live in the Autumn Realm for a while?"

Energy ripples through him, and he runs his fingers through my hair. "I could show you the Shimmering Shroomery, where the mushrooms grow as tall as trees. There's also Blackwine Forest. The Shrine of Nymphia is so beautiful at sunset. And if you consider your library to be big, then wait until you see mine. We have the largest library in all the realms—"

"Whatever did I do to make you think I'm interested in libraries?" I poke him in the cheek.

"You were interested in what I gave you beneath the table that one time." Farron crawls further onto my lap, bringing his lips to my ears. "The Great Scriptorium of Alder has plenty of hidden places."

My body heats at the memory: his soft mouth, my fingers

clenching the stone table, knowing people were browsing only stacks away. I feel my cock grow hard against his hips.

"You're distracting me," I growl.

He pulls back a little. "We could frame it as a diplomatic trip to my mother and your brother. A Summer embassy?"

My stomach drops because my brother would fucking love to send me there. No matter how we phrase it, he'll see it as his plan succeeding.

I can't go.

Not because I don't want to spend more time with Fare. Of course I do. I fucking adore him. But going with Farron means angling myself toward something so much more than I am here.

It's not an embassy trip.

I'd be stepping into my role as consort of the High Prince. Fuck, Damocles would love it. One day, sooner rather than later if Fare's mother has any say, I'll be living at Castletree, still in Damocles's shadow.

That's when it'll all fall apart. All the High Princes and Princesses of Castletree will realize I'll never be as strong as Damocles, never as smart as Farron.

Farron will see me for the fool I truly am.

I'll never belong at Castletree.

Why can't it always be like now? Fare and I, and the waves and the sand, and hearing him call out my name as we make love over and over again.

But that's not the destiny the gods laid for him, a future High Prince.

"Day?" When he says my name like that, tilting his head so brown locks fall across his brow, I feel weak.

Which is the last thing I need to be.

"I'll talk to Damocles about it," I say.

And the smile that lights up his face is brighter than the damn sun. "Really?"

"Really."

We kiss, falling back to the sand. His hands run down my bare chest, hips driving against mine.

"Fuck, Fare," I moan, nipping at the tender skin below his ear. "If we start this, we'll have to navigate home in the dark."

"I don't care," he breathes, fingers reaching beneath the top of my waistband.

I brace myself on the sand, and my palm scrapes something sharp. "Ow! What the—"

Farron's eyes widen, and he pulls his hand back, inches away from grabbing my cock. I can't help but let out a frustrated groan.

He gives me a playful smile and grabs the sharp thing that cut me. "I almost forgot. I was making this."

In his hands are shells and a piece of red sea glass strung onto twine. He flushes, running his thumb over it.

"That red piece is from the treasure we found," I murmur. "Did you find it in my room?"

"Yes, when you were sleeping, I noticed so many of the shells that washed up, and they were so beautiful. And I put them together, and it's, uh… It's for you."

"For me?"

He bites his bottom lip, eyes downcast. "Yes."

I clutch his jaw and force him to look up at me. "I love it," I tell him before kissing him again and turning around.

He lays the string of shells across my chest before tying it at the base of my neck.

"This way"—Farron places a kiss on the top of my shoulder—"even when we're in the Autumn Realm, you'll never be far from home."

# 22

## FARRON

ayton's hand looks so large as he runs it over the necklace. A strange feeling swells in my ribs. He's wearing something I made.

He takes in a long breath, then grabs me by the back of the neck and pulls me against him. Sunbaked warmth spreads through me as our skin touches. It's like during this last year, Day has unlocked something inside me. How could I never have realized how good this feels? There's a whole side of life I haven't known. Or more so, he taught me how to live.

And it's not just the sex, which is, admittedly, my new favorite hobby, even beating out my old favorite: cross-stitching. But Dayton has shown me that doing scary things isn't always the worst.

Especially if he's beside me.

Plus, he's grown fonder of the library, even if it is only to find the most secluded corners of it.

"Day." I breathe his name like it's oxygen, because to me it is.

He pushes me down to the soft sand, our bodies tangled. I hook my leg over his hip and feel his hard length press against me.

"I don't know if we have time," I gasp. "The tide."

Already, the foamy water laps at our feet. Soon, there will hardly be any sand on this little isle at all.

"It can wait," Dayton growls, shoving his tongue in my mouth before pulling away, tugging on my bottom lip with his teeth.

"You can't control the ocean, Day."

"For you, I can."

Something flashes in those blue eyes, wilder than a storm, deeper than the ocean's depths. And I know I'll never make it to shore again.

His gaze narrows, like he wants to ask what I'm thinking, but he must already know.

*I'm in love with you, Daytonales, Prince of Summer. All the stars and the sun and the moon could vanish from the sky, and you would be all the light I'll ever need.*

His lips part. He brushes his knuckles along my cheeks.

*Did you hear me? Please, hear me.*

"Your freckles look so cute in the sun," he murmurs and captures my lips. Slowly, carefully, like it's our first kiss.

"Make love to me, Day."

He kisses the column of my throat, biting and sucking. The intensity of our movements grows. Dayton's hands are everywhere, sliding over my skin.

Each kiss, each touch, ignites a fire within me. My fingers roam over his back, feeling the taut muscles. My world narrows to a wavering haze of salt and sun and him. The sound of the waves crashing around us barely breaks through my desire. His lips trail down my bare chest, tongue dipping into every indent of my stomach, before his fingers work on the knot of my clothing.

My cock twitches, and my breaths come in quick, heated gasps. I clutch the sand beside me, wet from the tide.

With nimble fingers, Day unwraps the fabric around my waist and throws it to the side. He sits up, and my entire body burns under his gaze.

"Damn, you're beautiful," he says.

A wave washes over, completely soaking us, before receding.

Dayton laughs and leans closer. The water is warm, but not as warm as his mouth as he wraps around my length and sucks.

This, he doesn't do slowly, taking me so far in his throat, I feel the muscles clench around my cock.

"Oh fuck, Day," I cry out, before another wave soaks us.

Smooth, wet sand slides beneath my heel as I arch my spine. His pace increases, his other hand tugging on my balls, sending a shiver through me.

Blinking up at the sun, all I can feel is his touch, taking me close to the edge.

"I'm going to come." I tangle my sandy fingers in his hair, then force his head down, needing him deeper. "I'm going to come in your mouth."

The low growl reverberating in the back of his throat is all the answer I need to buck my hips in a frantic motion as I fuck his mouth. His whole fist closes around my balls, and his tongue presses hard against my cock, lips suctioning in a truly mind-rattling feeling. I stiffen and then explode.

Day groans, the muscles in his neck bobbing as he swallows my pleasure. His eyes roll back. He releases me, pink lips shining, and crawls on top of me.

Dayton's fingers entwine in my hair, drawing me closer as he kisses me, and I taste myself and the salt of the sea.

He breaks the kiss for a moment, his eyes meeting mine, dark with desire. "Farron," he whispers.

I cup his face in my hands, pulling him down for another searing kiss. Our tongues dance, the taste of him making me dizzy with want. I can feel his heart pounding against my chest, a wild rhythm that mirrors my own.

Another wave douses us. His golden hair sticks to his jaw, pearls of water glistening over his body.

"How are you still dressed?" I reach between us to unknot his wrap.

The white fabric falls away and gets carried out with the next pull of the tide. We exchange a bone-deep laugh.

"A problem for later." Dayton smirks, pumping his arousal in an incredible display. His hand is huge, and yet his cock is still massive within it.

I lick my lips. "You'd always be naked if I had my way."

"That could be arranged, Little Leaf, but then you'd be aware of how hard my cock is every time you're in my presence."

"Every time?"

He gives me a dangerous look then fists both our cocks together. I grow hard again. With his other hand, he circles my entrance, preparing me.

"You have no idea. I watch you doing mundane, but unfortunately public tasks, and imagine bending you over and taking you—hard."

Drops of precum pearl on my tip.

"Fuck me, and hurry." The tide falls away less and less, water pooling in the soft sand around us.

"Anything you want."

He lifts my hips and sinks into me in one smooth, spellbinding motion. Another roaring wave splashes over me, completely drowning out my cry of pleasure.

Dayton throws his head back, golden hair sparkling in the fading sun's light. "I'll never get tired of this, fucking never."

He moves, powerful hips driving deep, the curve of his cock hitting every glorious nerve. "You better not, Day."

His grin is lopsided, roguish, and all fucking mine. He leans down, sliding even deeper, and captures my mouth.

As the waves wash over us, it becomes harder to breathe, the salty water mingling with our gasps and moans. But I don't care. All that matters is this moment. I feel him everywhere, his touch, his taste, his very soul merging with mine.

The water is up to my shoulders, and when I throw my head back, it's entirely underwater. "Day, the tide," I sputter as I sit up.

He pants. "Too fucking bad I'm not done with you yet. Good thing I can hold my breath a long time."

The Summer Prince spins us so I'm on top, hands pressing into his chest as the waves submerge him. As the tide swirls around us, I continue with movements as frantic as the ocean. The pressure of the water, Dayton below me, the heat and the cold, all blend into a single, overpowering sensation.

He rises out of the ocean and kisses me. My legs wrap around his waist, the waves swirling around us.

"This has been the best summer of my life," I gasp.

He clutches my face. "Farron, I—"

A wave crashes over us then, so loud it drowns out everything else. When it falls away, his lips are over mine and the words lost with it. But I imagine he said, *I love you.*

And I kiss him back like he did. Move my body with his like he told me those words.

Dayton's hands roam my body, finding every sensitive spot and setting it alight with his touch. I arch into him, moving in sync with the rhythm of the waves. His lips find mine again, the kiss deep and all-consuming, and I lose myself.

His hips move slowly, drawing out our pleasure, his other hand stroking me beneath the waves. The water rises higher, soaking us through, but we're oblivious to everything except each other. Dayton's every touch, every kiss, drives me closer to the edge until I'm teetering on the brink of ecstasy.

"Ready, baby?" he whispers in my ear.

Whimpering, I nod, burying my face into his shoulder. His skillful hips buck once, twice, until he reaches that sensitive spot deep within me. I come undone. His hand closes around my cock as I spasm into another wave of pleasure. His groan is loud and long as he releases deep inside me. The intensity of it leaves me breathless, clinging to Dayton as the world spins.

Teeth nipping my ear, he growls in broken, shattered words. "Gods, you feel so good. You make me feel so good. I fucking love coming inside you, baby."

Tears flow down my cheek, and I kiss his neck tenderly as we stay locked together.

Dayton's lips find mine once more. I surrender, letting the waves of desire and the tide carry us both away.

*I love you, Day. I love you so much. I'd do anything in this world for you.*

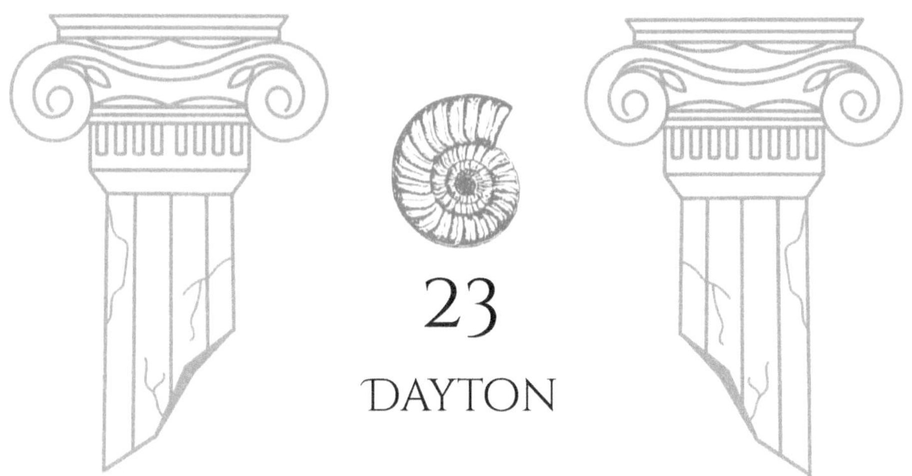

# 23

## DAYTON

I stride through Soltide Keep, the familiar halls doing little to lift the heavy feeling in my chest. The glimpses of my haphazard appearance in the tidepools seem to mock me as I make my way to the High Prince's chambers. I need to talk to him. Though I'm not sure as to what end. To ask his leave to go to Autumn? Or to beg him to present an acceptable reason for me to stay in Summer?

What happened on the isle with Farron, the manner in which we'd fucked on the beach. Had that been the start of something new or a goodbye? Had I heard him right between the rush of the waves? *Did you say those three words to me?* Or has my imagination gotten the best of me again?

My hand hovers over my seashell necklace. I don't know what choice to make.

After we'd made our way back to shore, I'd taken a revealing walk through Hadria with naught but a palm frond as coverage. Once we'd arrived at my personal quarters, I'd thrown on a beige tunic and loose pants. Farron had fallen into my arms, kissing me wildly, saying how excited he was for us to depart for Autumn tomorrow. Then he left to pack.

And here I am before the High Prince's chambers to ask him something. I still don't know what.

As I linger outside the door, I hear voices through the crack. I adjust my stance and peer through to see Damocles and Decimus in deep conversation.

"You must have noticed how much time they were spending together," Decimus says.

Damocles gives a long sigh. Despite the late hour, my brother is still dressed in his fine regalia. Stars, I wouldn't be surprised if the bastard sleeps in it.

"He kissed the Autumn Prince in front of the whole court," Damocles says. "I'd be a fool not to notice that."

A slight chuckle from Decimus. "Why the frown, brother? Was this not your grand plan?"

"Unfortunately, this summer has only proven how unready our youngest brother is."

My stomach drops, and I force myself to stay still.

"Instead of courting the Autumn Prince properly," Damocles continues, "he has stolen him away in shadows and night. Instead of staying in the palace and learning from his High Prince and the High Princess of Autumn, he has frolicked in the Pirate Isles and slept with the goats up on Mount Tempitus."

My heart sinks. I press closer to the cool stone wall.

"Furthermore, he's too cocky in the arena," Damocles adds. "Always showing off. He's late to events—if he bothers to attend at all."

"He's not much better when he does show up," Decimus's voice cuts in, low and sardonic. "You remember the Winter Equinox three years past? How he got so drunk, he challenged Winter's vizier to a duel? Nearly started a war over a petty insult."

The memory stings. That old, blue-lipped fae was a jerk and had needed a good ass-kicking. I had been so sure I was defending our honor, but thinking back... How foolish had I looked?

Damocles sighs and rubs the bridge of his nose. "I thought a union between Farron and Daytonales would ground him, make him see reason. But he'll end up embarrassing Farron like he does the Summer Realm."

Decimus places his hands flat on the table. "I believe he's quite fond of the Autumn Prince now."

Damocles shakes his head. "Those feelings will pass. He never stays with one partner for long. Besides, Daytonales is more than aware of what a union with Farron will mean."

"What is that?"

"He would be expected to be a leader," Damocles says, his tone dripping with frustration. "He's not ready for that. He doesn't understand what it means. Dayton is a fool—"

Their words slice through me. I step back, unable to bear any more. My brothers' voices fade as I turn and retreat down the corridor, my head spinning.

I make my way to the gardens, needing the open air. Taking a seat on a bench, the vibrant flowers seem like a mockery.

I thought I was doing well. I thought my time with Farron meant something. But to Damocles and Decimus, I'm still a reckless child, unfit for responsibility.

*Isn't that what I wanted? The freedom to explore Summer with no care in the world?*

I bring my hand to my chest. The burning beside my heart flares up again. I lean forward, burying my face in my hands.

*Dayton is a fool.*

I look up at the moon, heart beating painfully. *What do I do?*

Then, I realize this choice has nothing to do with me.

It has everything to do with Farron and what's best for him.

And it sure as fuck isn't me.

# 24

## FARRON

Carefully, I tuck the last of my books into my trunk before slamming the lid closed. Mother has Eleanor trapped in the chair before the wicker vanity and is fussing with her hair. Nori sighs and continues staring into the jar of fish bones she's collected over our time here.

I look around the room. Despite the oppressive heat and always shaking salt or sand out of my trousers, this place has felt like home. Every memory is a treasure, from long dinners over rich wine, to exploring caverns filled with shining sea glass, to…to him.

It all comes back to him.

Even the more uncomfortable memories can't dampen the experience. Like the time Nori went up to Dayton's mother, Princess Sabine, and placed her small hands upon the princess's pregnant belly. "This child will be a princess of blood and sand," Nori had said confidently. "She will raise armies and sink cities into the depths. She will be of air and water, and all will fear her."

Well, that had sent Sabine into hysterics, and Mother had been mortified. Nori had been forced to sing an ancient Autumn hymn at dinner one night as penance, and we were all squirming in our seats with embarrassment.

But besides that, the long months in the Summer Realm have passed as a dream. And although I'm sad to go, something else flutters in my chest.

Excitement.

A new chapter begins. Now, I'll get to show Dayton my home. And whatever this is between us—this magical, terrifying, beautiful *thing*—may flourish in the land where all things come to die.

I catch Mother staring at me, her eyes soft and smile sweet.

"What is it?" I ask.

"You seem different," she says. "Lighter." She walks over to me and places a hand on my shoulder. "It's a good thing."

I smile inwardly. Maybe she's right. Something about Dayton has changed me, and I don't think I'll ever be the same.

I grab my satchel and click open the latch—

"Argh!" A giant green bullfrog leaps out, nearly landing on my face, and I hear a cackle of laughter from the doorway.

Anger rushes up my chest to the top of my ears. "Dom! Billy!"

I sprint after them, ignoring my mother's calls.

They chuckle and dash ahead, but I'm quicker than them. They lead me through the corridors of the villa before they turn around a corner. I skid after them to see they're huddled behind Decimus for protection. He laughs and ruffles their hair.

"I'll be sorry to see you little Autumn leaves go," he says. "We all will be."

Another secret smile plays at my lips. Because it doesn't feel like goodbye. It feels like the beginning of something wonderful.

My family gathers in the entrance hall of our villa. Outside, our carriage, carved with acorns and chestnuts, looks too dark for the bright sun and green foliage of the Summer Realm. Dayton's three parents arrive to wish us well, as Damocles and Decimus quickly join their side.

Something flits in my stomach. *Where's Dayton?*

The mothers are hugging, Decimus is squeezing both my brothers in a bear hug, my father is shaking hands with Ovidius, and Cenarius is being forced to look at Nori's jar of bones.

I walk up to Damocles. "Where's Dayton?"

A tic fires in his jaw. "You know Daytonales by now. He's never where he's supposed to be."

That feeling in my stomach is moving up, clenching at my lungs, weaving around my heart. "But he's supposed to come with us. He said he'd talk to you."

"What do you mean?"

"He's going to come with us to the Autumn Realm," I say in a breath. "He's going to come with me."

Pity flashes in the High Prince's eyes. "I'm sorry, Farron. He never spoke to me about this."

No...no. No. It can't be like last year. Things are *different*. I've changed. Mother said so.

Hasn't he changed too?

Damocles must see the pain in my eyes because he places a hand on my shoulder. "It's clear you care for my brother. So, I'll tell you the same thing I told Decimus last night. Dayton is a fool."

A retort builds inside me, but I bite my tongue because who am I to defend someone who won't even keep his word?

"Dayton is a fool," Damocles says again. "But I know my brother. His spirit is wild and untamed, like the fiercest of Summer storms, yet there is a warmth and a light in him that can shine in any darkness. He may stumble, he may falter, but within him lies the potential to ignite a path of glory."

So, his brother has seen in Dayton what I have then. "I fear Day doesn't believe that about himself."

"I thought for a long while it would be me to ignite that flame inside him, then perhaps a partner. Possibly someone we do not even expect. But as he is now, Daytonales is an unchecked fire, one whose path I would caution to stay far away from."

Stay away from Dayton? The notion feels impossible.

I sprint out of the villa, hearing my family call after me. But I don't stop. I have to find him. It's not possible after all the days in the sun, the nights lying on the sand, skin to skin, heart to heart, that he would just...let me go.

I run under the peach trees, the once-bursting fruit now withered. Where is he?

Tinkling laughter fills my ears, and I spin, catching sight of the stables. Two fae women totter out, their bare bodies barely hidden by a horse blanket. They catch my attention and giggle. "He's still too drunk to fuck. Pretty to look at, though."

Now the feeling carves its way up my spine, filling my head with rushing blood. I careen forward and push open the door to the stable.

Lying in the straw, surrounded by empty wine bottles, and fully naked, is Dayton.

He looks a mess, golden hair tangled, dark circles under his eyes, a stinking pile of sick in the straw beside him.

He pulls himself up to a sitting position, and his eyes are cloudy as he registers me. "Fare?"

I stagger backward, catching myself on the wall. "Day…"

Then, Dayton does what Dayton does best. He laughs. "Looks like I had a bit too much fun last night."

I can barely breathe, let alone speak. "We…we're leaving today."

"Oh?" Dayton rubs his hands over his eyes. "Right. That's this morning."

"I thought you were coming with me."

Dayton's whole body stills. His head pitches forward, face covered by golden hair. "Of course I'm not fucking coming with you, Fare." He looks up at me, his mouth unfamiliar. No smile. No cocky smirk. Instead, a harsh frown cuts across his face. "We have fun, you and me. But this isn't one of your silly books. You're a dreamer." His eyes shimmer. "And you need to leave me out of it."

"Dayton…"

"You don't belong here, Farron," he snarls. "And I sure as fuck don't belong with you."

All summer, I'd watched Dayton fight. Fight in the arena. Fight against Justus. Fight for me.

I'd said Dayton had changed me. I have to fight too. Fight for him, for us.

But Mother was wrong. I was wrong.

Because I'm not a different person. I'm still the coward I always was.

I turn and run.

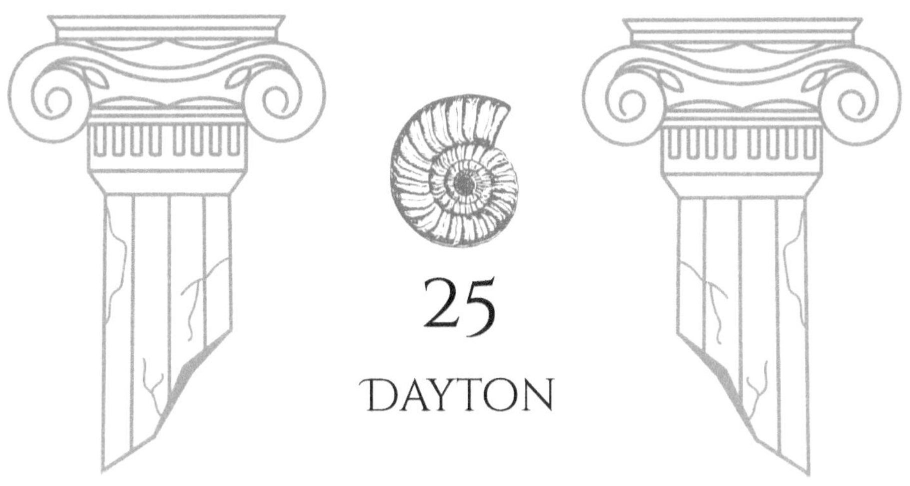

# 25

## DAYTON

It's because of summer's heat, we get autumn. It burns, and it burns, and it burns, until it withers everything into ashes.

*That's what I did to you.*

But now, as the carriages drift away, there is no flame beside my heart.

I don't feel anything at all.

# 26

# EPILOGUE – FARRON

The halls of Castletree are alive with merriment. There is much to celebrate. I peer through the crowd of nobles in the ballroom to look at the four thrones. Sabine stands beside Damocles, who sits on the Seat of Summer. She holds the new Princess Delphia. This celebration of the Rainbow Eclipse Festival at Castletree is Sabine's first official outing since Delphia's birth.

And like he promised, Dayton is here. Not that he's said a word to me since I arrived. Presently, I can see he's well into his cups and chatting to a gaggle of young Winter nobles.

Castletree's ballroom is done up in grand splendor, as always, a symphony of nature and magic. Soaring arches and pillars carved from the living tree reach toward the open windows and starry sky. Vines and delicate blooms twine around the columns, their petals glowing with light.

In the center of the room, the guests twirl in dance, their laughter and music ringing out, bringing to life the magic I always feel in Castletree.

I turn my attention back to the dais with the four thrones. My gaze slides from Day's family to the Spring throne, the huge chair backed in blooming pink flowers and green vines. The newly crowned High Prince Ezryn sits stiffly upon it, metal fists clenched.

My stomach flips. The Spring Realm is so secretive I've only heard rumors, but word is his mother, the former High Princess, died passing on her Blessing. It's a rare occurrence, but it has happened before.

Further, rumor has it that the family experienced another loss: Kairyn has been banished to serve Queen's Reach Monastery atop Mount Lumidor, where acolytes dedicate their lives to worshipping the memory of our lost queen

I resist the urge to slink off to Castletree's library to research it more. It's smaller than the Great Scriptorium of Alder, but I've always found it a comforting escape when I've stayed here with Mother. There's something cozy and warm about it, and the Autumn Wing always feels like home.

Worry clouds my heart as my gaze shifts to my mother. She locked herself in her room for days after word came of Isidora's passing. On the third day, she emerged, stone-faced, appearing to have aged a decade in that time. She didn't speak to any of us about it, but I see the grief in her eyes.

"Everything alright?" a deep voice says behind me. I stiffen as a hand clasps my shoulder.

I spin to find the tall Winter heir.

"Oh, hi, Kel—uh, Keldarion," I peep, then swallow with a dry throat. "I was thinking about Ezryn. It must be hard for him."

Keldarion gives a long sigh. He wears a cloak of shimmering satin lined with white fur. His doublet is sapphire with glittering thread. Atop his head is a silver circlet with a single blue gem at the center. His light eyes narrow as he looks up to the dais. I know he and Ezryn have been close since childhood, so losing Spring's High Princess must have hurt him as well.

"It is," Keldarion says. "He's been staying with my parents and me for a time now. He does not like to speak of his feelings, though. I often wonder what's going on inside his head."

Gingerly, I place my hand atop Keldarion's, which is still on my shoulder. "Everyone deals with grief in their own way. I'm sure knowing you're there for him is a comfort."

Keldarion gives a low laugh, then ruffles my hair. "Such wisdom, little prince. Did you read that in one of your books?"

"Uh, yeah. Maybe." I swallow. "But there is happiness here too. The birth of Delphia. And if it's not too bold, are the rumors true you intend to propose to Lady Tilla this night?"

The Winter Prince stiffens, and I worry I've said too much. But then he gives a gruff sigh. "I believe those rumors were spread by my mother herself, and since I'll do anything for her, then…"

All at once, I feel a kinship toward Keldarion, despite us being worlds apart. Perhaps he too is not ready for the throne, and this marriage is another step toward it. My gaze settles on his mother, Princess Runa. Her dress looks crafted from the finest sapphire velvet, and a shimmering crystal necklace adorns her throat. She's beside Keldarion's father, Erivor, the High Prince of Winter, who sits upon the Seat of Winter like he owns all of Castletree.

"Just the two royals we were looking for," a low, deep voice slurs. A voice that travels to my very core.

Dayton stands before us, arm slung around Kel's intended, Tilla. Her cheeks are flushed, and she laughs at his words.

"I found this maiden all alone on the dance floor," Dayton continues. "Pray, where be her handsome prince?"

Tilla *tsks*, her long black hair falling from her tight-knit bun. I wonder how much wine these two indulged in before they located us.

"I've been looking for you forever, Kel." Tilla narrows her eyes. "You aren't avoiding me, are you?"

Kel paints a perfect smile on his face and grabs her arm. "Of course not, dear. I was catching up with Prince Farron. You've met him before."

Tilla blinks her big eyes at me. "Oh, yes. Dayton has been talk—"

"You should give your date a dance, Kel," Dayton interrupts, boldly slapping Keldarion on the arm.

"I do not partake in dancing," Keldarion says. "Besides, I think what she requires most is water and rest."

Keldarion leads Tilla toward her lady's maids.

And that leaves me alone with Day. The last thing I wanted to happen today.

"Fare," he says lowly.

Why does his voice have to sound that way? Why does it make my whole body tremble? One look in his blue eyes, and I'm a ship lost at sea.

"I have to go." I step away.

"Can we talk?" He grabs my arm. "Somewhere alone?"

"That's the only place you like me, isn't it? In the shadows."

A muscle feathers in his jaw, and I know he's suppressing a retort.

I sigh, so weak where he's concerned. "Follow me."

We leave Castletree's grand throne room, and I lead him to my favorite place. When we enter the library, the air changes. It's crisper, tinged with the earthy scent of fallen leaves and the rich aroma of old books.

"Can't say I've ever been here," Dayton says.

The library unfurls before us like a dream. Shelves stretch up toward the vaulted ceiling, crafted from amber wood. Books, scrolls, and artifacts fill the shelves. Living vines intertwine with the shelves, their tendrils winding around leather-bound tomes. Moonlight filters through stained glass windows.

Cozy fireplaces are scattered throughout, casting a golden light with their flames. I can't hear the festivities in the throne room anymore, just the crackling logs. Above us, autumn leaves fall. Their colors are vibrant—deep reds, burned oranges, and golden yellows.

Dayton picks up a leaf between his thumb and forefinger. "It suits you."

"What does?"

"Castletree. This library. You're meant to be High Prince."

*Castletree could suit you too,* I think, but keep the thought to myself, inhaling a deep breath. The air carries the perfume of aged parchment, polished wood, and the faint spice of cinnamon and cloves, emanating from the perpetually brewing mulled cider in a corner.

I lead him to a comfy couch in front of the fire in a secluded alcove.

Dayton falls to the cushions, his tension seeming to ease now that he's away from the celebration. He thrives on people, large conversations, and crowds, but he needs this too.

"You wanted to talk," I say, breaking the silence, "so talk."

He opens his mouth, closes it.

"What?" I sneer. "Is the great gladiator for once at a loss for words?"

"I miss you."

My heart melts, because that's been my only thought since I left Soltide last summer. But I keep my expression neutral, unable to look at him as I say, "You didn't *have* to miss me."

*If you'd come to Coppershire.*

"See, that wouldn't have worked either, Fare," Dayton says. "That would be all politics. It wouldn't be like the summer. Fun. Damn, I miss the *fun* we had together."

I observe him from beneath my lashes. There it is, the thing he can't get past. My title. My future.

"I can't have fun forever. My mother is eager to pass on the Blessing and—"

Dayton stands, and he's in front of me, not touching, but close enough I'm enveloped in the scent of salt and sea and sunshine. "Not at this very moment. You could have fun now."

I take a step away from him. "My mother expects me to find an acceptable consort. That doesn't bother you?"

He shrugs and closes the distance I just created. "You don't have one now. I could show you lots of ways to have fun. We could go to taverns together. Share a woman. Attend parties with the sole purpose of fucking from dusk to dawn. The possibilities are endless."

I don't want any possibilities but him. Though he's probably already lost himself in countless lovely bodies from the Summer Realm since I last saw him. I don't step away again, mind reeling. He still wants me. Well, wants me some of the time. Will that be enough? Is having only a small piece of the Summer Prince better than nothing at all?

Slowly, I rest my fingers over the shell necklace I made him. He's still wearing it. His breath hitches beneath my touch.

"If," I say, "I want you, then you must come. You drop everyone else and come to me. Could you do that?"

"I could do that," he says, voice sparking with the first bit of life all evening. "If…"

"If?"

"If you say you want me right now."

I pause, taking him in. Tall, golden hair, tan skin, a little broken around the edges, like a priceless chipped relic. And I know this plan is foolish, because I don't want a little of him. I want him all. "I want you."

"Fare." He grips my face and pulls me into a searing kiss.

The wave that's been drowning me the last few months recedes, and I let out a loud moan into his mouth.

Day moves away and chuckles. "Knew you still wanted me."

"Can't believe you would doubt that." I grin back and throw myself into his arms, wrapping my legs around his waist.

He holds me up, hands tangling in my hair, mouth sliding down my neck where he nips on the sensitive skin.

The fire crackles beside us, casting dancing shadows across our bodies. Dayton sits up, his blue eyes longing. He leans in, his lips brushing against mine with a featherlight touch. It sends a shiver down my spine, and I melt into his embrace.

Our kiss deepens, growing more insistent. His hands travel over my back, drawing me closer. We fall to the couch, sinking into the plush cushions. Our lips never part.

"Tell me, Fare," he gasps, "how often do people come here?"

My heartbeat grows wilder. "Hardly ever."

He presses his lips to my cheek, and I feel the smile there. "Perfect. Though, I would do this with an audience. I've been waiting too long to have my fill of you to let anything stop me."

His hands are everywhere, unbuttoning my vest, slipping beneath my tunic. I mirror his movements, pushing the strap of his toga off his shoulder. With his chest bare, I trace every hard line of his muscles.

Dayton's kisses grow more urgent, more insistent, as if he's trying to pour all his emotions into his touch. My heart races in response, and I feel a rush of heat that has nothing to do with the flames beside us.

Dayton grips the bottom of my shirt, and I help him, tugging at the hem until the fabric slips over my head and falls to the floor. He pauses, his eyes drinking me in, and then his lips are on mine again, more fervent, more desperate.

My fingers find the knot of his toga, and I fumble with it. He laughs and throws off the entire thing, leaving himself naked.

"You don't wear anything beneath that?" I laugh.

"Why add another layer to having you?"

I fall against him, the warmth of his chest against mine intoxicating, and I can't help but sigh into his mouth.

We move together, a flurry of eager hands and breathless kisses, until he's stripped me of my pants. The heat of the fire blazes over me. I lie on top of him, and he touches my mouth.

Parting my lips, and without breaking eye contact, I suck his finger.

"Tell me, Fare," he says, "were you with anyone else these last months?"

I let my teeth scrape against his skin, and he hisses before pulling away and circling my entrance.

"Only someone I'm courting would be privy to such knowledge."

He narrows his gaze. I want to ask him the same thing, but I won't do that to myself.

"Fine," he says and slips a finger inside me. "I think I'd like to watch you with a woman. Would you like that, Fare?"

I grit my teeth as glorious pleasure erupts through me. Pleasure only he's ever given me. "With you, as well?"

"Of course."

"Then yes." He slips a second finger inside and my vision turns hazy. "Yes, yes, yes. Oh gods, you feel so good."

He captures my cries with a kiss, and I feel his cock harden against mine. I arch my hips, and then we're moving in perfect rhythm, cocks sliding together as he works me.

I might explode from just this.

"Give me more than your hand, Day."

He pushes me on my back. The couch molds to my body, and he leans over me, looking like a sculpted god. The firelight makes his hair shimmer like melted gold. I grab his cock, stroking it lightly, slippery with precum, rubbing the prominent veins beneath my finger.

"Always so hard for me." I grin.

"You can bet I'll be at every event to do this. Know the moment you see me, my cock will be raging to be inside you. That I'll find the first fucking moment and drag you away to stuff you full of my cum. No matter how pretty you're dressed up." He nods to my finery scattered on the floor.

My entire body feels like an electric current. Desperately, I grab his forearms. "Inside me, *now*."

"Of course, Little Leaf."

He lifts my hips and angles the tip of his cock at my entrance. Then waits, looking down at me.

He's so still, staring at me like he sees more than an awkward prince who isn't even worth courting. "Why are you hesitating?"

"Savoring the moment." He sighs. "I thought of this every night as I pumped myself into oblivion."

My body trembles at the thought of the powerful Summer Prince alone in his bed, body trembling with visions of me. I blow the hair off my forehead. "What if I told you I did the same thing?"

"Oh, fuck, baby." He strokes my cock. "What a naughty boy in your room, taking yourself in your hands, getting your sheets all sticky, thinking of me. Tell me you screamed my name."

"I screamed your name."

"And you'll scream it now." Day slides into me.

The movement is fluid as he sinks all the way to the hilt, my body spasming as I adjust to his size. He curls over me, forehead to forehead, golden hair brushing my cheeks.

"Does it hurt?"

"No," I whimper, clenching around his cock, wishing we could stay this way forever. "I love the feeling of you inside me."

"Me too." He kisses me, then licks my cheek, before bracing a hand on the back of the couch. He begins to move, *really* move.

Each powerful, long thrust causes my entire body to shake. The sensation of Dayton within me, the way we fit together so perfectly, is overwhelming. I cling to him, my fingers digging into his shoulders, anchoring myself as wave after wave of pleasure crashes over me. "Yes, Day. Yes."

How could I have ever thought there was any other choice? I could never deny myself even a sliver of this. Just fun—that's what he wants.

But he's not fucking me like I'm his friend or like some random fae he met at a bar. The kisses along my neck, the desperate cadence of my name whispered over and over in the rhythm of his hips, how his eyes shine with what might be tears... He's fucking me like he *loves* me.

Maybe I'm delusional. A romantic. A dreamer. But I know deep inside, I'm waiting for him to realize what I already know, what our bodies already know, what he has scorched inside my heart. He loves me.

He loves me.

And if this is all I have for now, it'll be enough. I'll fuck him like I love him, every time. Because I do.

I wrap my legs around his hips, drawing him deeper. Slide my tongue along his collar bone, tasting the salt of his sweat.

"Whose great idea was it to do this in front of the fire?" he gasps, hair flying across his brow.

"Yours."

"Always blaming every bad idea on me." He smiles, and it's so bright I nearly die.

"The bad ideas are usually yours," I say.

"Not you, though." He grips my cock, stroking in time with his thrusts. "I can't hold on much longer, Fare."

"Don't."

We lose ourselves in one another, our movements growing primal as we chase that final, blinding crescendo. My cock twitches, so ready for release.

"Day, Day, Day," I gasp.

"Almost, baby." He throws his head back, powerful muscles in his neck straining. Another thrust, so deep inside me that my stomach flips. Then another and another. I can't hold on.

"I'm coming, Day."

He bursts within me. It feels like the world shatters and re-forms. My cock twitches in his palm, ropes of cum shooting between us. I fall, trembling, clutching him. His head sinks to my chest.

We lay entwined for a long while, heartbeats still wild. My breath feels shaky as he moves, kissing my chest, my neck, my cheek. "Fare. Fare. Gods, you're beautiful, baby. You feel so good."

Delirious. He sounds delirious.

Doesn't he know that this is so much better than he could find in a tavern for one night? Or maybe I'm wrong. It's not like I know.

He's all I've ever had.

Day presses a gentle kiss to my forehead, my fingers trailing lazily up and down his spine. "You're so beautiful, Fare," he murmurs, the words a soft caress against my skin.

*I love you,* I whisper in my mind, feeling the truth of it settle deep within me. But outside, I push him off me and grin. "You're right, that *was* fun."

His smile falters before he laughs. "Come on, let's clean up. I have a promise I need to keep."

OUR ABSENCE WAS NOT NOTED, the celebration still in full swing. Dayton and I make our way to the drink table as we try to rehydrate from our exhausting rendezvous.

"Be right back," Day says and drifts into the crowd.

I look around the ballroom. Keldarion is exchanging harsh whispers with his parents. He releases a sigh and turns to the crowd.

"Hey, Little Leaf." Dayton taps me on the shoulder, and I turn to him. "My promise."

"What promise?"

Dayton shifts awkwardly from foot to foot; I notice he's got one hand tucked behind his back. "I got you—"

"Attention, everyone." Keldarion's voice booms across the ballroom. The music fades, and a hush falls over the crowd. I glance around, noting the anticipation on everyone's faces.

Runa looks every bit the proud mother, her icy elegance softened by a rare smile. Erivor stands tall and imposing, a look of satisfaction etched on his features.

Keldarion clears his throat. "Thank you all for joining us tonight. I have an important announcement to make. For some time now, I have been courting Lady Tilla." He pauses, allowing the weight of his words to sink in.

A hush spreads over the crowd, a mixture of curiosity and excitement. I glance at Dayton, who raises an eyebrow. Keldarion continues, "Lady Tilla has shown me the depth of her strength and grace, and I am honored to have her by my side."

I gaze back at Tilla, standing among some Spring nobility. Her expression is inscrutable, eyes fixed on Keldarion. There's something in her posture, a tension that belies the calm mask she wears.

He's going to propose, I realize, like he mentioned earlier. To me, a proposal should fill the air with celebration and warmth, except it feels like the entire ballroom might freeze. In fact, by Keldarion's feet, thin lines of ice creep out.

Keldarion takes a deep breath, his gaze steady. "Tonight, I wish to—"

A high-pitched scream erupts from outside the ballroom, and the whole place ripples with panic.

Keldarion steps forward, his expression hardening with determination. "Stay in the ballroom. I will investigate. Ezryn, with me. High Prince Damocles, Father, and High Princess Niamh, protect the people."

"Damn." Dayton's mouth falls open. "Commanding the High Rulers, and he's not even in charge of Winter yet."

The High Prince of Winter draws a glittering sword. "Go, my son."

Keldarion rushes beside us, Ezryn following closely. "You two, with me." He points at us.

Dayton staggers to the side with the movement, and I glimpse a rose falling from his hands. It gets crushed beneath the soles of the other guests, but I tear my gaze away and follow Keldarion.

We rush out of the ballroom, closing the large doors behind us, and make our way to the main entrance hall. Some of the staff and guests have pushed themselves against the walls, trembling. The main door to the castle is opened, and beyond, I see the true outside of Castletree, the grounds and the bridge that leads to the forest. But before the door is a slumped mound of black cloth.

Keldarion holds out his arm, and we all slow behind him.

"I d-didn't mean to make such a sound," one of the servants says, a middle-aged fae woman with a pink apron around her large hips. I recognize her from my visit to Spring last year.

"It's alright, Marigold," Ezryn says, his voice reverberating within his metal helm. "What happened?"

She clutches a hand to her chest. "I was bringing some fresh tea to the party and suddenly the doors blew wide open! And in swoops this m-monster!"

I look back to the mound of cloth on the floor. Strange vines—no, not vines, but briars—are tangled in the fabric. Blood pools beneath.

"That's not a monster." Keldarion advances. "It's a man."

"Kel, wait—" Ezryn says.

Keldarion kneels and grips the black cloth. Ezryn rushes forward. Dayton gives a shrug before he grabs my arm and tugs me behind him.

Carefully, Keldarion rolls the figure over, and the breath catches in my throat. I'm not sure what I was expecting...but it wasn't him. A beautiful fae with long dark hair strewn across his brow and thickly lashed eyes. But how can I think of him as beautiful when he's in such a state? Red blood lines his lips, and deep scratches mar his hands. He's wearing nothing but rags. Even so...there is an unearthly quality about him.

Keldarion's eyes blaze with blue fire. "Who are you?"

The fae reaches up a shaking hand before it falls from Kel's silver circlet down to his jaw, leaving a bloody trail. "My name is Caspian," he says. "I escaped the Below. I need your help."

Thank you so much for reading Prince of the Arena! We hope you enjoyed your adventure in the Summer Realm.

Reviews help others find our book. They are vital to authors. If you could take a moment to leave a review on Amazon and Goodreads, it would mean the world to us!

You can leave a review on Amazon here:

You can leave a review on Goodreads here:

# Acknowledgments

We are so grateful to have had the opportunity to explore Dayton and Farron's backstory through the pages of this novella.

Thank you to our friends and family for their constant love and support. A massive hug goes out to our beta readers for helping us make the Princes of Summer and Autumn shine.

Thank you to Elise for capturing Dayton and Farron with her beautiful art.

A huge thank you to Team Briar. Mom, Dad, Graeme, Lisa, Stacey, and Zara — we couldn't run the Vale without you.

With endless gratitude, we would like to thank our newsletter subscribers who read the first version of *Prince of the Arena*. And to our readers, thank you for loving Dayton and Farron as we do.

# BEASTS OF THE BRIAR DELUXE EDITONS

We are so excited to share that Bloom has officially acquired the print-rights to Beasts of the Briar and deluxe paperback editions with sprayed edges are coming!

Pre-order the deluxe editions here:

# About the Authors

Elizabeth Helen is the combined pen name of sister writing duo, Elizabeth and Helen. Elizabeth and Helen write fantasy romance and love creating enchanting adventures for their characters. When they're not writing, you can find them snuggling their cats, exploring their rainforest home in British Columbia, Canada, or rolling the dice for a game of Dungeons & Dragons. You can connect with them on TikTok, Instagram, or Facebook.

**Facebook Readers' Group**

Join our Facebook Readers' Group to interact with like-minded bookish people, get behind-the-scenes info on the creation of our books, receive sneak peeks for Book 5, and chat all about the Enchanted Vale and the fae princes!

facebook.com/groups/elizabethhelen

AuthorEizabethHelen.com

facebook.com/elizabethhelenauthor

instagram.com/author.elizabeth.helen

tiktok.com/@authorelizabethhelen

amazon.com/author/elizabethhelen

goodreads.com/elizabeth_helen

# Also by Elizabeth Helen

**Beasts of the Briar**

Bonded by Thorns

Woven by Gold

Forged by Malice

Broken by Daylight

*Novella*

Prince of the Arena

## Join Our Newsletter

Join our newsletter for an exclusive behind-the-scenes look into our writing process and sneak peeks of the Beasts of the Briar series!

*Read the scene where Caspian first meets Rosalina—through his eyes.*

Get an exclusive villain POV bonus scene when you sign up for our newsletter. Join now to claim it!

ElizabethHelen.SubStack.com

www.ingramcontent.com/pod-product-compliance
Lightning Source LLC
Chambersburg PA
CBHW020806310726
48969CB00002B/726